Kissinger didn't hear the other man

His eyes were riveted on the photo of the weapon that had been found at the scene of a brutal mass murder just outside of Birmingham. The gun was a modified Browning automatic complete with a built-in silencer and flash suppressor.

Cowboy's heart was doing calisthenics. There had to be some kind of mistake. He looked up at Kurtzman, waiting for an explanation.

"What is it, Cowboy? You look like you've just seen a ghost."

"Maybe I have," Kissinger managed to whisper, looking back down at the photo, still trying to make sense of it all.

"How so?"

"I know this gun," Cowboy explained quietly. "It's one of mine...."

Mack Bolan's

ABLE TEAM

ABLE TEAM

COWBOY'S REVENGE

Dick Stivers

A GOLD EAGLE BOOK FROM

WORLDWIDE

TORONTO • NEW YORK • LONDON • PARIS
AMSTERDAM • STOCKHOLM • HAMBURG
ATHENS • MILAN • TOKYO • SYDNEY

First edition December 1987

ISBN 0-373-61233-8

Special thanks and acknowledgment to
Ron Renauld for his contribution to this work.

Printed in Canada

PROLOGUE

Thurmond Cates liked to take his family down to an isolated offshoot of Alabama's Cahaba River on weekends. It was a chance for them to be together, away from the squalor of their cramped home in the trailer park just outside the city limits of Birmingham. There, alongside the clean, rushing waters, they could spend a carefree day together, enjoying one another's company without having to contend with the park's other tenants. Their neighbors were a constant source of annoyance, either with their loud, unruly behavior or their inevitable requests that Thurmond, a first rate handyman, take a look at some broken or malfunctioning appliance they hoped to have fixed without having to pay a repairman. After putting in a fifty-hour workweek as head maintenance man at Birmingham Central High School, Thurmond didn't care to spend his Saturdays and Sundays in similar pursuits, unless of course they had to do with the trailer he and his family of six called home.

"Now, check out the pro in action," Thurmond teased his oldest son as he cast his fishing line into a bend in the river where the current ran slow, blocked partially by a fallen oak tree and topped with a sprinkling of lily pads.

Twelve-year-old Uland watched diligently, eyes on the baited hook sweeping through the air, end over end, guided by the thin, translucent line until it plopped neatly in the water a few feet from the nearest pads and cat-tails. The hooked worm slipped beneath the surface, sending out rippling waves in widening circles, creating a target for the red-and-white plastic bobber that followed it, marking the spot Thurmond had told his son he was aiming for.

"Wow! How'd you do that, Dad, huh?" Uland shook his head in disbelief. "Shit, every time I try it I end up in the damn lily pads!"

"Watch your tongue, boy," Thurmond chided. "You want your mother hearin' you talk that dirt?"

"She can't hear this far," Uland said, glancing over his shoulder at a picnic table set in a grassy clearing fifty yards away. His mother and grandmother sat on either side of the table while two children played around the edge of a nearby campfire.

"I don't care if she can't hear you," Thurmond insisted. "You shouldn't be usin' foul language, period. Cursing's a lazy man's excuse for a vocabulary, and I won't truck it from you, understood?"

"All the kids at school are always cussin'."

"That don't make it right." Thurmond sat down next to his son on the river's embankment, putting them on the same eye level. "Look here, Uland. Your teachers all say you got a full load of brains between your ears, and I expect you to make use of 'em. I swear on the grave of my own daddy, you're gonna be more than some two-bit school janitor when you grow up."

The young boy sighed. It wasn't the first time he'd heard this lecture, and he was sure it wouldn't be the last. Sometimes he wondered if being successful would be worth all the pressure and sacrifices that seemed to come with it. One thing he knew for certain: even if he reached the top, he wouldn't give up times like this, being with his family down by the river. Of course, if he had a lot of money he sure as hell would make certain they moved into a nice house a lot closer to the water than that rat-trap trailer park they lived in.

"Okay, okay, don't go mopin' on me." Thurmond reached out and nudged his son. "Come on, get a line in so's we can see who gets the first bass. Loser's gotta clean the whole catch."

Uland turned his attention to his own bamboo pole, baiting a fresh worm to the new hook he'd had to resort to after loosing the previous one in the cattails. The worm, a fat crawler he and his younger brother had caught by flashlight the night before, squirmed wildly on the hook, trying to shake itself free.

"This time I'm gonna do it," Uland vowed, standing up and testing the pole's sway with a few practice casts. His lips closed with tight determination, and his eyes focused on the spot near the lily pads where his father's bobber floated.

"That's it. Concentrate, get a feel for that pole. Let it know who's boss," Thurmond advised. "When you're ready, let that bait fly nice and smooth. Not so herky-jerky like last time, hear?"

Uland nodded and took one long, deep breath before cocking his arm back, then snapping it forward in a fluid motion that approximated the form he'd seen his father use a hundred times before. Unlike most of the other times, however, this cast produced results similar to that of the older man, and Uland let out a squeal of glee when he saw his cast land between Thurmond's bobber and the half-submerged oak.

"All right!"

"Good job, son. I knew you could do it."

Uland sat back down next to his father, grinning from ear to ear. Thurmond patted him on the back, then propped his pole between his knees while he rummaged through his coat pockets for a pipe and a small pouch of tobacco.

Moments later, as his father's familiar smoke mingled with the fresh outdoor scents of the riverside, Uland thought to himself, Goddamn, this is great. . . .

"JUST LOOK AT THOSE TWO, MAMA," Vera Cates said as she watched her husband and son fish along the bank.

"Two peas in a pod, that's them," Gram Cates replied, glancing up from the patchwork quilt she was working on. When she smiled there was a gap where two of her teeth were missing. "That Uland's gonna do you proud, Vera, mark my words. He's a fine, fine boy."

"I know it, Mama." Vera gestured to the nearby fire, that grew as the two younger children fed twigs to the flames. "I've got three fine children."

"Soon as you can quit with your braggin', we got ourselves a quilt to finish."

"Yes, Mama." Vera rubbed her eyes, then cleaned her bifocals on the soft cotton of her skirt. Noticing that the two youngest children were leaning too close to the flames, she called out, "Jimmy, Lottie, that's enough now. You can watch the fire if you want, but stop throwing things into it or else it'll be too hot for your pa to cook the fish."

The children whined in protest, but retreated a few steps and sat cross-legged before the fire. Jimmy shot a quick glance toward the river, then snickered to his sister, "They gotta catch some fish 'fore they can cook 'em."

Vera rummaged through her sewing basket until she found a spool of thick green thread. She checked the color against the design she was working on. Satisfied with the match, she threaded a needle and began humming to herself as she went back to work. Her mother picked up the tune, and together they lent music to the song of birds nesting in the thick brush that surrounded the clearing.

Hand-stitched quilts were a family specialty dating back to the days of the Civil War, and both Gram's and Vera's work equalled their predecessors. They turned out blankets prized throughout Jefferson County and other parts of the state where their reputation had earned them a number of commissions. The quilting was tedious, painstaking work, but neither woman complained. Both had a quiet patience about them, and took pride and consolation in the knowledge that their efforts produced enough additional family income each year to help provide not only for the children's everyday needs but also for their future education. Like Thurmond, the Cates women had resigned themselves to the modest life-style of their trailer home, but they wanted to make certain that future generations would have a fighting chance to escape the tangles of poverty.

The tranquil harmony of the setting was soon disrupted by Uland's excited yelps at the river's edge. He stood up and gently jerked back his fishing pole, which had bent sharply only seconds before. Thrilled to have caught the first fish of the afternoon, Uland waved away his father's attempts to coach him in reeling the catch ashore. This was his big moment, and he wanted the glory all to himself. He continued to cheer himself on as he worked the pole and reel, playing the fish.

"Man, it's a biggie, Pa! Catfish, I'll betcha!"

"Could be, son. Could be."

Back at the picnic site, the women and children watched Uland. With their attention diverted to the shoreline, they failed to notice the sudden appearance of a man who had quietly stepped clear of the thickets. He was tall and gaunt, with a thin, pallid face and eyes the color of a washed-out sky.

In his hand was a gun.

The man was less than ten feet away from the picnic table when Vera Cates noticed him out of the corner of her eye. She turned to face him and was just opening her mouth to issue a cry of alarm when he pointed the gun at her face and pulled the trigger.

With a muffled sound no louder than a cracking knuckle, a 9 mm jacketed bullet ripped through Vera's throat, stifling her cry and taking her life with it as it exited through the back of her neck. The woman toppled to one side, landing awkwardly on the quilt she was stitching. Her severed artery spewed jets of crimson onto the white cloth, startling Gram Cates, who had seen her daughter slump forward without realizing why. The elderly woman's back was turned to the gunman, and a second shot shattered her skull before she had an opportunity to see her killer.

Jimmy Cates was only eight years old, but he had seen enough gunplay on television and even on the streets near the trailer home to vaguely comprehend what was happening. He called out to his mother and grandmother as he rose to his feet and intuitively placed himself in front of his younger sister. Gram Cates had fallen, and she lay still on the ground, her body twisted awkwardly. The man stepped around the picnic table and stared across the campfire flames at Jimmy and Lottie.

"You shot Gram and my ma." Jimmy's voice was petulant, accusatory.

"That's right, nigger boy. And you're next."

Two shots, fired in quick succession, felled the two children. Jimmy's knees gave out as a bullet perforated his heart, and he tumbled headlong into the fire, giving off the vile smell of burnt hair and flesh. Lottie died sitting down, her childish eyes wide with amazement and confusion, a fatal wound discoloring her light brown cheekbone.

Although both Thurmond and Uland had heard Jimmy's initial exclamation, neither had bothered to look at the clearing. Uland's full attention was on his pole and the jerking bobber that slowly made its way back toward him as he reeled in his line. The water was clear, and soon both he and his father could see the youth's catch, a mature striped bass still darting from side to side, scales gleaming in the sunlight.

"That's a biggie, all right," Thurmond said, reaching for a net propped against the boulder beside him. He caught a glimpse of the man who was walking calmly toward the embankment, gun in hand. Cates froze in place, dumbfounded.

"Hey, get the net ready, Pa!" Uland almost had the fish out of the water, and he was leaning forward to grab the line where it fed out from the end of his pole. "Pa, hurry it up!"

But Thurmond was oblivious to his son. His eyes were fixed on the man and the gun now pointed at his chest. Behind the intruder he quickly noted the slain members of his family, and even though a part of his mind refused to believe what he saw, the bulk of his instincts were already marshaled to a more immediate cause, that of self-preservation. The fishing net was already in his hand, and he tightened his grip on the aluminum shaft, gauging the distance between himself and the man with the gun.

Too far. He had to try to buy some time.

"Preacher Carruthers, why—?"

Thurmond's question was silenced by five quick, muffled shots from the gunman's pistol. Thurmond twitched, taking each of the bullets in the chest. The net dropped from his fingers, and he staggered to his left in a feeble attempt to shield his son from the next volley. Dead on his feet, he collapsed into the river, landing close to the still-struggling fish and snagging his arm on the taut line. Seconds later, Uland splashed lifelessly into the water, his body also riddled by the strangely quiet bursts of gunfire. The bass tugged at the untended line until it managed to shake itself free of the baited hook, then swam clear of the reddening water where the two bodies floated eerily in the faint current.

The man stood on the embankment, watching his last two victims, relishing the surge of exultation he'd felt when he'd first pulled the trigger back near the picnic table. At long last he had his revenge, and it felt wonderful, better than he had ever thought it might.

"Die, niggers, die," he murmured at the drifting corpses.

When the river had claimed the bodies of Thurmond and Uland Cates, the man turned and walked slowly back to the picnic site. The sun had just slipped behind the Sand Mountains, and there was a noticeable drop in temperature as shade crept across the clearing. He paused near the fire and held his breath against the stench of Jimmy's seared flesh as he warmed his gloved hands over the dying flames. It was an overpowering smell, however, forcing him quickly back up from his crouch. Before leaving the picnic site, he dropped the emptied pistol near the fire's edge. He had no further use for it. Of course, if his vengeance did not seem to be complete enough at some point in the future, he had other guns, just like this one, waiting and ready to be used. He gazed contemplatively at the weapon now lying in the dirt next to Jimmy and smiled to himself as he recalled the providential twists of fate that had put the gun at his disposal.

Satan's will. That's what it had been. Harlan's new master had proven to be a far better provider than the God he'd worshipped before.

"His will be done," Preacher Carruthers whispered as he walked off into the thickets from whence he had come.

1

Set deep in cold Virginia soil, the basement beneath the lab at Stony Man Farm had by nature the harshest indoor environment of any structure on the 160-acre compound that served as command post for the nation's most elite and secretive special forces. Although a furnace was encased in one corner of the subterranean enclosure, consuming fuel and belching heat through ducts that reached up to the weapons and electronic labs overhead, little of that generated warmth was relegated to the basement itself.

Not that John "Cowboy" Kissinger minded.

Stony Man's resident weaponsmith did a portion of his work in the upstairs laboratory, but he preferred the privacy of the basement workshop. Most of the year there was enough heat generated by his bench lights and the assorted power-driven tools of his trade to keep him comfortable. During those few instances when the chill became too extreme, there was always the small Franklin stove next to the workbench. It was a cast-iron, potbellied anachronism that fed on small chips of cured pine and oak from the Blue Ridge Mountains that provided a scenic backdrop for the isolated, clandestine outfit.

Tonight, with temperatures dipping into the low thirties and a possibility of snow in the forecast, a fire was crackling in the stove, visible through grating vents in the fuel door that looked like the teeth of a Halloween jack-o'-lantern.

On top of the stove was a built-in hot plate, upon which Kissinger had set an equally old-fashioned coffeepot. Once the water inside the pot was hot enough, it began to geyser up through the main stem and percolate back down through a mound of freshly ground beans. Kissinger smiled with anticipation as he smelled the heady aroma wafting from the pot.

"Right with you, java. Business before pleasure."

After dinner at Stony Man headquarters, a short jaunt away from the lab building, Kissinger had come back to the workshop to continue work on his latest modifications of the Barrett M-82, a key weapon in the arsenal of those who risked their lives on the orders of Stony Man's in-house director, Hal Brognola, who in turn took his orders from men of high position in the nation's capital. Rarely did a month go by without one of the special forces requesting this semiautomatic rifle capable of firing .50-caliber Browning machine gun cartridges, the most powerful ammunition available for a weapon that size.

One of the rifle's other strong points was its relative portability for a weapon with so much power, but John Kissinger was a perfectionist. There was no such thing as good enough, and he'd been spending the better part of the past month trying to come up with a way to make the gun even lighter and shorter than its present design without sacrificing anything in the way of performance. With meticulous care he'd trimmed away at excess bulk and replaced certain metal parts with wood, fiberglass and other less dense material that could withstand the stress and abuse of the rifle's merciless firing power. Many of his replacement parts hadn't stood up under testing at the farm's firing range, but overall his efforts had skimmed almost four and a half pounds off the Barrett's normal thirty-five pound weight, and he'd shortened the length to under sixty inches. True, nobody was suddenly going to be able to hide the bastard inside their coat when they went out gunning for the scum of the earth, but as Able Team member Carl Lyons was fond of pointing out, in this type of work the line between life and death was sometimes measured by ounces and millimeters. When your ass was on the line, you went with anything that might bump up the odds that you'd fight another day.

Wrapping up his stint at the workbench, Kissinger took care to clean the various files and rasps he'd used that day, rubbing them across a file card that scraped off even the smallest wood and metal particles to ensure continued precision. After hanging the tools up in their appropriate brackets on the wall above the bench, he dusted off the other equipment—variable drill press, propane torch, bench vise, mounted grinder, polishing wheel and the felt-gripped cradle that held the partially disassembled Barrett's stock.

Most of the items in the basement had been there when Kissinger had joined Stony Man Farm as successor to Andrzej Konzaki, the operation's previous crack weaponsmith. Kissinger had bought a few additional items over the past months to round out the workroom, and he was finally feeling as if it were truly his own area. Maybe one day it might even live up to the memories of his first shops—the one in Brooklyn where he'd first learned the craft from his now-deceased father, and a cramped cubicle up in Wisconsin where he'd first cut his teeth as a free-lance weaponsmith after leaving the Drug Enforcement Agency. He'd had some great times back then, doing specialty work for various reputable armorers

when he wasn't busy tinkering with a few original prototypes. Who knows, he thought, where his work those few
years might have taken him if it hadn't been for a tragic
fire that had destroyed the entire building his Wisconsin
shop was located in and claimed the lives of three people, including his partner, Howie Crosley.

Kissinger rode the swell of nostalgia as he poured
himself some coffee and tossed a few more wood chips
into the Franklin. There was an old oak rocker near the
stove, and Kissinger eased his muscular frame into the
chair's comfortable embrace. He spent a few minutes
rocking, letting the coffee mug warm his hands as he
stared into the flames and recalled that much larger Wisconsin fire that had so radically altered his life. He
thought that he had managed to put that incident out of
his mind, but it had taken only this slight provocation to
bring the images rushing back with all the accompany-
ing emotions he'd felt back then—grief over the loss of a
friend and partner; despair that all those months of work
had gone up in smoke...

All right, all right, enough of this crap, he finally
chided himself. Who'd he think he was, some old-timer
with his best years behind him, resigned to mulling over
the "good times" that had somehow passed him by?
Hell, no. It would take a damn sight more than a few gray
hairs and a fortieth birthday lurking around the corner
to put Cowboy Kissinger out to pasture. Fucking-a, anyway. He had his hands full keeping tabs on the present
and future without diddling away his time on strolls down
memory lane.

He left his chair long enough to go to a file cabinet and
track down a spec sheet on what was shaping up to be his
next pet project once he'd finished streamlining the
Barrett M-82.

The FOG-M, brainchild of the Army Research Development and Engineering Center, was being touted in many military circles as the most revolutionary weapon to hit the conventional battlefield in years. Its abbreviated name stood for Fiber-Optic Guided Missile. In essence, it was a five-foot-long projectile with a camera in its nose capable of transmitting images back to a launch operator by means of a sturdy, unreeling cable made of highly sensitive optical fibers. The operator, viewing the missile's progress on a video monitor from within the concealed safety of a launch truck, would be able to hone in on a target merely by maneuvering a joystick that could change the missile's course. In principle, the operator was a glorified video game player, with the crucial difference being that when he successfully guided his cable-connected warhead to its intended target, the destruction viewed on the screen would actually be taking place somewhere within its ten-mile firing range.

The army intended to use the FOG-M primarily as an antitank weapon with additional applications for battling enemy helicopters. Kissinger saw its potential as a vital ace for Stony Man agents to have up their sleeves when they went up against terrorists who were known to cover their asses with enough firepower or backup fortifications to discourage basic assault tactics or other countermeasures.

As with the Barrett rifle, Kissinger's first priority—if he were able to get his hands on one of the FOG-Ms—would be to make the missile a leaner, meaner piece of hardware, requiring less storage space and a shorter setup time. With all the peripherals attached to the system in terms of computerized programming, the use of the fiber-optics cable and other high-tech advances, he also knew that this would be a project requiring the assistance of two other key players at Stony Man. Aaron Kurtzman, the compound's ace communications expert, knew all there was to know about computers, and Able Team's Hermann "Gadgets" Schwarz had earned that nickname for his astonishing ability to fathom the way almost any piece of machinery worked and how it could be made to work better. Kissinger also knew that both men were currently available. Kurtzman seldom left headquarters, and Schwarz was back at the Farm along with the other members of Able Team after their most recent assignment.

Kissinger finished his coffee and closed off the stove grating before he locked up for the night. Upstairs he found a couple of staff workers still in the lab, going over inventory figures from a recent count of armaments and ammunition in the Stony Man stockpile. Hal Brognola insisted on knowing the weapons inventory at all times. He also did not believe in being overstocked. A good portion of John Kissinger's time was often devoted to figuring out ways to increase the efficiency of warehouse-stored weapons or ammunition that other aboveboard military agencies would merely file away and forget should they ever threaten to become obsolete in the face of some new, improved product.

In a similar vein, Kissinger's contacts at Army Research had already caught wind of rumors that the FOG-M project was in danger of being scrapped because of in-house politics and calls to redesign the missile, adding so many new-fangled extras that it would be rendered inoperable. Crap like that reminded Kissinger of how lucky he was to be plugged into the Stony Man operation. Here there was a limited chain of command, and he knew where he stood at any given moment. There wasn't that angst he'd felt during his own three years with the Army

Department of Weapons Testing and Design back in the seventies, when any number of pencil-pushing geeks were capable of pulling the plug on whatever project he might be working on.

Kissinger briefly scanned the inventory report and traded a few words with the staff workers before heading out into the cold. Clouds filled the night sky with the promise of snow. Kissinger trekked across the grounds to the main building, which, like all the other above-ground structures on the premises, was deliberately drab and inconspicuous in appearance, built to pass as an outbuilding of a rural Virginia estate. A camouflaged airfield was tucked behind a stand of conifers a few hundred feet off to his left, and although it seemed as if he had the grounds to himself, Kissinger knew that his every movement was being monitored by security forces strategically placed along the Farm's periphery as a security precaution.

"Hey, Cowboy!" Rosario Blancanales called out when Kissinger walked in through the back entrance to the main building. "Decided to crawl out of your hidey-hole and join the real world for a few minutes?"

Blancanales was in the pantry, hauling down a box of canned goods from an upper shelf. Slightly shorter than Kissinger and a good twenty pounds lighter, he nonetheless cut an imposing figure in his corduroy slacks and wool sweater. Despite a big-boned frame that made him seem stocky, he was known among his peers for his agility and quickness, attributes that had served him well growing up in the barrio and later as a paratrooper in Nam. He flashed the endearing, good-natured grin that was part of the reason the others called him "Politician." "Stick around long enough and you'll get a chance to sample my famous chili."

Kissinger made a face and shook his head. "Thanks, Pol, but I'm gonna pass. Lyons told me the last time you made that shit his tongue went numb for a week."

"Yeah, and we all know about Lyons's taste. You've seen some of the women he's taken out. They're hardly—"

Before Blancanales could finish his wisecrack, a human blur swept out of the kitchen, bowling him over and sending the cans flying. Kissinger took a quick step back to avoid being struck by sixteen ounces of kidney beans and watched as Carl Lyons wrestled Blancanales to the floor.

"I heard that, you bastard!" Lyons seethed between rabbit punches to Pol's midsection. Carl was closer to Kissinger in size, and it seemed at first that Blancanales was overmatched. But as the two men struggled their way out of the pantry and into the wider confines of the dining room, the scrappy Hispanic managed to wriggle his way clear and laugh at the man who had blindsided him.

"It was supposed to be a compliment, *amigo*. Lighten up."

"That part of my life's private!" Lyons retorted.

"You mean privates, don't you?" Blancanales smirked. He reflexively threw his arms up in front of his face to deflect the can of tomatoes Lyons hurled at him.

"Keep it up, Pol, and you're going to end up the secret ingredient in that goddamn chili of yours, got it?" Lyons was only half joking. Blancanales turned to Kissinger for sympathy.

"Hey, Cowboy, why don't you haul this guy down to your basement and see if you can't fine-tune his sense of humor."

"Tell me something, Blancanales," Lyons said. "How many of your lady friends have you buried lately?"

Pol didn't have a humorous comeback for once. The playful sense of mirth left his face, replaced by a look of concern and apology.

"Sorry, homes," he told his partner. "I wasn't thinking. What a mouth I got...."

Kissinger didn't have to be reminded of Lyons's situation. He'd seen the chip that the Ironman had been carrying on his shoulder since the death of Julie Harris, the second woman close to him who'd been killed in recent months by enemy forces. And before that there had been Flor Trujillo. Losses like that weren't easy to shrug off, even for someone with an exterior as hardened as that of Carl Lyons. A blowup like the one that Kissinger had just witnessed was inevitable. Cowboy was actually surprised it had taken this long. Julie had been killed two missions ago.

"I mean it," Blancanales apologized again. "I was way out of line."

"Forget it," Lyons said, exhaling. "Besides, I got a little carried away. My fault as much as yours."

"If that's the case," Pol said, holding out his palm, "how about we call it even?"

Lyons slapped Blancanales's palm, and all three men picked up the scattered chili ingredients. Kissinger gestured toward a doorway leading to the main facilities. "I'm looking for Gadgets. He in there?"

Blancanales shook his head. "He and Brognola flew into Washington to pick up Phoenix Force. Guys just got in from Beirut this afternoon. After they get debriefed, they'll be coming here for a powwow."

"What's new in the Middle East?"

"Same old shit with a few new twists," Pol said. "We'll get the full picture later, but apparently the Shiites are making a move here in the States."

Lyons had finally calmed down enough to show off his grin, which always seemed to hold more menace than Pol's. "Well, if they do, you can bet your sweet ass we'll show up to be their travel agents."

"How's that?" Kissinger asked.

"We'll see that they get one-way tickets to Allah," Lyons vowed.

Fixings in hand, Blancanales stood back up and headed for the kitchen, telling Lyons, "Come on, Ironman, help me whip up this batch. Be a good boy and I'll let you lick the spoon when we're finished."

"They call me Iron*man*, Pol, not Iron*gut*," Lyons taunted.

Kissinger left them to their culinary misadventures and passed down the hall to the main facilities of Stony Man Farm, trading acknowledgments with an internal security officer on his way to the far end of the corridor. The computer room and communications center were located adjacent to each other in a kinship similar to that between Hal Brognola and Aaron Kurtzman, guiding forces behind much of what went on behind these deceptively ordinary-looking walls.

Kurtzman was at his favorite post, before a bank of consoles in the computer room. Totally engrossed in his duties, the computer wizard reminded Kissinger of one of the members of Emerson, Lake and Palmer, a band he'd subjected his eardrums to fifteen years ago. When he wasn't fighting off the bombardment of decibels coming from the mountains of speakers at the edge of the stage, Kissinger had begrudgingly admired the dexterity of keyboard player Keith Emerson, who had spent most of the concert flawlessly cavorting between no less than five different instruments. There was a vague similarity to Emerson in the way that Aaron Kurtzman seemed to simultaneously peck at the controls of a half-dozen computers with single-minded concentration. But there the resemblance ended because, despite his confinement to a wheelchair, the burly hacker looked more like a cross between a trained grizzly and a retired professional wrestler than a wiry rock musician. And his computers were much quieter than mellotrons and synthesizers.

"Got a minute, Bear?"

Kurtzman held up a finger, motioning for Kissinger to wait as he finished programming a few last commands, his eyes still fixed on several monitors flashing data on their softly glowing screens. Then he turned his attention to a printer and checked to make sure a supply of paper was properly linked to the tractor feed before speaking. "Funny thing you should drop in, Cowboy. I was just about to track you down myself."

"Yeah?"

The Bear nodded, cuing up the printer and starting it. A high-pitched whine filled the room as a dot matrix printing head raced across the blank page, filling it with text and visual diagrams. A nearby telex began to spit out a ream of documented paper, passing along news Kurtzman had managed to tap into while doing one of his routine searches of supposedly classified transmissions of various law-enforcement agencies throughout the nation.

"Came across an interesting item over the wires down in Birmingham," Kurtzman told Cowboy. "Looked like something that might perk up the ears of a gun nut like you. Here, take a gander."

Kurtzman ripped a sheet from the telex and handed it to Kissinger along with the data from the computers. Most of the information had to do with a mass murder that had taken place along the banks of the Cahaba River just outside Birmingham. An entire family of blacks had been gunned down at a site where they had been picnicking. There were no suspects in custody as yet, but the apparent murder weapon had been found at the scene. It was an unfamiliar weapon, modeled somewhat after an old Browning automatic pistol but vastly modified to include such features as a built-in silencer and flash suppressor. A photo of the gun was being circulated on a top-priority, top-secret basis to all agencies that might be able to identify the manufacturer and make of the mystery weapon.

"What'd you want to see me about, anyway?" Kurtzman asked.

Kissinger didn't hear the other man. His eyes were riveted on the duplicated photograph, and deep between his ribs his heart began doing calisthenics, cheered on by a jolt of adrenaline. There had to be some kind of mistake. The Bear was playing a prank; that was the only explanation. He looked up at Kurtzman but saw no glimmer in the man's eyes to indicate he was being ribbed.

"What is it, Cowboy? You look like you've just seen a ghost."

"Maybe I have," Kissinger managed to whisper, looking back down at the printouts still trying to make sense of it all.

"How so?"

"I know this gun," Cowboy explained quietly. "It's one of mine."

2

Hal Brognola's cigar smoke drifted across the table toward Aaron Kurtzman. Cowboy Kissinger ignored it as he completed his mental roll call of the men sitting in Stony Man's conference room.

The trio responsible for taking on those "sensitive" domestic assignments that official government agencies were reluctant to tackle for fear of unwanted and unfavorable press coverage was obviously anxious to get back to work, to return to the jungle as Lyons often put it. Carl Lyons, Rosario Blancanales and Hermann Schwarz had, over the years, logged more miles across the U.S. of A. than traveling salesmen with frequent-flyer passes. They efficiently—and often brutally—dealt with any obstacle that might otherwise put a crimp in the average American's guaranteed right to life, liberty and the pursuit of happiness.

"Madre de Dios, amigos," Blancanales cracked as he looked around at his comrades. "It looks like the family's all here. So where's our next vacation?"

Hal Brognola stared at Able Team's resident comedian with a grave eye. "Let's not waste our time on wisecracks, Pol, okay? Few of your missions have been holidays."

"Yeah, yeah."

Kissinger paid little attention to the banter as he doodled on his writing pad. His thoughts were elsewhere, however, back roaming through the cerebral files of yesteryear....

IT WAS EARLY 1982.

He'd just completed five years with the DEA, working primarily as a government-sanctioned storm trooper in the war against those thriving off the illegal trade in drugs. Although he'd found a certain satisfaction in putting drug kingpins out of circulation and in closing down more border smuggling operations than he could ever hope to remember, it wasn't the kind of work that was closest to his heart.

Looking back over the years since he'd traded a pro football outfit for military togs in the bloody quagmire of Vietnam, Kissinger decided he'd experienced his greatest satisfaction in the mid-seventies when he'd worked in the army's Department of Weapons Testing and Design. Prior to the army job he'd dabbled periodically with amateur gunsmithing, no doubt because it had been a hobby of his father's back in their Brooklyn tenement. Once thrown into the profession on a full-time basis, it had proven to be a rewarding challenge, diminished only by the inherent bullshit that had come with being a part of a well-entrenched Pentagon bureaucracy. Kissinger expected that if it hadn't been for all the office politics and petty infighting, he might have stuck it out longer.

With some free time on his hands after burning out on yet another government job, Kissinger had decided to give free-lance gunsmithing a fling. His father had just passed away over the Christmas holidays, and all his tools were still in storage back in New York City. Cowboy had returned home to live for the first time since graduating from Brooklyn High School of Math and Sciences, partly to help his mother work through her grief and to help put her life back in order, but also so he could put in long, inspired hours in the old man's workshop. Once he'd brushed up on his smithing skills, he'd checked up on some of his old armorer contacts, lining up barely enough free-lance work with outfits such as Colt, Beretta and Heckler & Koch to earn a less-than-meager living. Although it was definitely a step in the right direction in terms of self-satisfaction, he longed to take the job one step farther. He wanted to have more time and resources at his disposal so that he could work on developing prototypes for a few original designs that he had first dreamed up on his free time while working for the army.

That summer he spent a weekend in Cambridge attending a ten-year reunion for the MIT graduating class of 1972. It was there that he ran into one of his old college roommates, Howie Crosley.

They had never really been that close during their university days and had only met each other through a mutual friend. Although the three men had shared an apartment a few miles down the road from campus, they had not socialized together. Looking to expand upon the degree in engineering he had received while on his football scholarship at Ohio State, Kissinger had taken his studies seriously. Crosley had been the archetypal party animal, always eager to abandon his textbooks in favor of a cold pitcher of beer and the warm embrace of an inebriated sorority pledge.

The one time the two of them had gone out had been the night Crosley's date had stood him up for the Emerson, Lake and Palmer concert. Kissinger had let himself get talked into taking her place, even though the only hard rock he'd ever cared for was the candy his dad used to buy for him when they'd spent Sundays at Coney Island. The concert had done more damage to Cowboy's ears than his entire tour of duty in Nam, and he'd taken care to avoid anything that Crosley had considered to be a good time for the rest of the semester they'd lived together.

Crosley had cleaned up his act in the intervening ten years. At the reunion he looked as if he'd swapped his *Rolling Stone* subscription for the guidance of *Gentleman's Quarterly*. Gone were the ratty jeans and T-shirts, replaced by a custom-tailored suit that complemented his short-cropped reddish hair, which had once been a billowing mess that had hung below his shoulders. He spoke with a calm, persuasive confidence, and if it hadn't been for the fact that he was wearing a name tag, Kissinger probably wouldn't have recognized Crosley at all.

As it turned out, the two of them struck it off nicely the second time around. They left the reunion for a late dinner at a posh Cambridge restaurant where Crosley wouldn't have passed the dress code ten years before. After leaving MIT, Howie claimed he'd returned to his hometown of Madison, Wisconsin, a place where he'd thought he could do a good job of being a big fish in a relatively small pond. Between party binges at the university he'd somehow managed to learn enough to land a job at an engineering firm run by his brother-in-law. His taste for liquor had nearly ruined his chances of advancement, and it was only after joining Alcoholics Anonymous that he'd taken the steps that had helped him assume control of the firm when his brother-in-law had chosen to retire. Crosley had also dabbled in real estate, making some choice property investments that had added to his income.

Being a successful businessman suited Crosley for the most part, he admitted, but the routine was starting to get to him, and he was primed for something new. When Kissinger explained his present gunsmithing work, Howie listened with intense curiosity, asking a horde of questions and finally issuing a not-so-modest proposal. If Kissinger would be willing to go partners, Crosley would provide Kissinger with an office and workshop in Madison, along with enough seed money that John could drop all his other free-lance work and concentrate exclusively on developing his own line of weapons. They shook on the deal right there at the table and ordered champagne to toast their new venture. Two weeks later Kissinger was at work in Wisconsin.

The first and foremost weapon Kissinger wanted to get off the drawing board was a semiautomatic pistol he proposed calling the QA-18, after the apartment address in Brooklyn where he'd grown up. Starting with a very basic design that most closely resembled a stripped-down Browning FN, Kissinger concentrated on adding extra features that would make the weapon more unique and versatile than the British model that had seen such widespread usage since World War II. Although he set out to make numerous overall refinements so that the resulting QA-18 would bear little resemblance to the Browning, three improvements were the most dramatic. By lengthening the butt and reformating the ammunition cartridge, Kissinger's pistol would carry fifteen rounds of 9 mm ammunition as opposed to the Browning's thirteen. To counter the extended butt in terms of weight and balance, Kissinger also set out to lengthen the barrel in such a way as to include a built-in silencer and flash suppressor.

No small task.

Days became weeks, which in turn became months, and still Kissinger wasn't able to come up with the right configurations in the design to make it both efficiently workable and economically feasible in terms of production. Several times he got as far as putting together prototypes for firing tests, but in each instance any innovation came at the expense of performance, usually in terms of accuracy.

Crosley stood patiently behind Kissinger and continued to fund the research and development, although a sense of obligation led Kissinger to go back to doing a little free-lance work so that he wouldn't feel so totally dependent upon his partner's generosity. During that time they saw each other frequently outside of work and developed a growing, if somewhat superficial, friendship held together primarily by their mutual business interests. When Crosley decided to try out marriage, Kissinger served as best man.

Eight months later Cowboy was able to take some of the sting out of his partner's quickie divorce by announcing that he'd finally worked the major bugs out of the QA-18. On a vibrant fall afternoon the two of them went out to the field behind the office building where Kissinger had done all of his work, and for the better part of an hour they took turns firing the prototype to see if it could stand up to long-term use. It did.

Ecstatic, the men celebrated far into the night, conjuring up grand plans for the future of their little baby. Neither of them had spoken publicly about the QA-18, not wanting to tip off any possible competition, but that would all change soon enough. As soon as Kissinger tidied up the design and did a little last-minute fine-tuning of the weapon, they would secure a patent on the prototype and contact various manufacturers to cut a deal for production of the weapon. Kissinger still had enough government contacts to line up sales for the QA-18, which he was sure would become a staple in the arsenal of the armed forces and numerous federal law-enforcement agencies eager to stand up to the increasingly potent firepower being used by the criminal element.

Fate, however, had other plans.

Eager to wrap up loose ends on the project as soon as possible, Kissinger and Crosley set aside the following Saturday for some serious overtime. They showed up at the office building shortly before dawn, cranked up on coffee and adrenaline, ready and raring to go. The only other people around were a night janitor and a five-man crew taking inventory at a chemical supply store that occupied most of the ground floor of the building.

While Kissinger settled down at his desk to go over blueprints for the QA-18, wanting to work out some of the problems on paper before tinkering further with the prototype, Crosley started on the patent papers in his office across the hall. A few minutes later Howie stuck his head in the door and said he was on his way downstairs to get more coffee from the vending machine.

Kissinger didn't remember how long he mulled over his designs after that, but it seemed only moments passed before he heard a massive explosion and felt the floor and walls of his workshop jolt, toppling file cabinets and shaking tools off his workbench. When he got to his feet, a second, more forceful explosion bowled him over. He struck his head on the edge of his drill press and blacked out momentarily.

When he came to, flames were surging across the carpet of the main hallway and licking their way into his workshop. Overhead sprinklers were squirting down jets of water that had little effect on the spreading blaze.

Drenched and stunned, he tried to grasp the gravity of the situation. The heat was already unbearable, and he knew there was no way he could venture past the flames in search of Crosley. He'd be lucky to save his own ass.

Struggling to his feet, Kissinger raced the fire to his blueprints. The fire won, devouring the sheets in seconds and starting on the drafting table. His bench was already aflame, and when he tried to grab the QA-18, the metal's heat scorched his hands. There was a foul taint to the smoke rapidly filling the room, and Kissinger suspected toxic fumes would snuff out his life if he didn't clear the room immediately. With the doorway blocked by a wall of flames, there was only one avenue of escape. Taking long, full strides, Kissinger dashed for the window and threw himself headlong into the glass, throwing his arms up in front of his face at the last possible second.

They called John Kissinger "Cowboy" because of a wild streak in his nature that only came into play during moments of intense athletic competition or life-and-death emergencies. He'd taken countless falls in his life—as a pro on the gridiron, as a warrior in combat and as a mountain soloist climbing sheer-faced cliffs without safety gear—but none of his tumbles matched the two-story drop to the concrete of a nearby vacant parking lot. How he managed to land without killing himself, much less breaking any major bones in his body, was a freak stroke of good fortune every bit as farfetched as the odds that had set fire to the building.

When Kissinger regained consciousness, he was being loaded into an ambulance in the parking lot. Less than an hour had passed, but where there had once been a lavish two-story office complex, there was now only a heap of smoldering rubble rising from the hose-drenched area.

Fire fighters were still putting out spot blazes. A couple of bodies—or what had once been bodies—had been found, one on the ground floor and the other in a collapsed stairwell linking the first and second stories. Immediate identification was impossible. However, Crosley's Jaguar was still parked in the lot. When the local coroner got his hand on Crosley's dental charts a week later, he was able to confirm what Kissinger had already deduced as he was being hauled away to the hospital for precautionary X rays.

Howie Crosley had gone up in smoke, as had all paperwork and prototypes for the Kissinger QA-18. Because of the high flammability of the chemicals on the ground floor, the blaze's heat had been so intense that the few scraps of metal to be found in what had once been Kissinger's workshop had looked more like dollops from a Dali landscape than parts of a gun.

Relying on memory, Kissinger had briefly attempted to recreate his dream pistol, but there were too many gaps, too much lost ground. Having come so close only to be thwarted was just too much for him to cope with ultimately. Cowboy's heart was no longer in it, and he turned his back on any hopes of putting out another original weapon. He took on more free-lance assignments with established firms and eventually did some work for the CIA that brought him to the attention of Aaron Kurtzman. He had quickly accepted the Bear's invitation to join Stony Man.

"Earth to Cowboy," Blancanales whispered, leaning across the table and elbowing the weaponsmith out of his reverie.

Kissinger's neck flushed with embarrassment as he looked around the room and saw some of the other men eyeing him curiously. He diverted his gaze downward and saw that he'd been sketching a rough semblance of the QA-18 pistol on his notepad.

"Anything wrong, John?" Brognola queried.

"No, no, I'm fine."

"Did you hear me?" Sure that Kissinger hadn't, Brognola repeated, "I got clearance for us to have a look at the FOG-M. Should be here by the end of the week. You think you might be able to go over it and see if we can't have it operative if the Hizbullah start making problems for us?"

"You mean when the Shiite hits the fan, right?" Blancanales said.

"I'll tell you one more time," Lyons warned Blancanales on behalf of the others. "Can the humor and put it back on the shelf."

"Yeah, next to the chili," Gadgets chuckled.

"It's getting late, gentlemen," Brognola said as he pushed his chair back and stood. "I think we've accomplished enough for one night. Let's adjourn before Able Team turns into the Three Stooges on us."

The men began filing out of the conference room, trading more jibes and good-natured putdowns. Blancanales might get razzed for his frequent wisecracking, but secretly the others were grateful for his comic relief as a way of releasing some of the pressure that came with their thankless and often frustrating vendetta against the many-headed beast that was urban terrorism. No matter how successful they might be on any given assignment, there was usually little time or breath wasted on celebration or self-congratulation. Lop one head off that vile hydra in one part of the country and another, perhaps even uglier one would rear in its place a state away. Now it was the Shiites and their brutal offshoot, Hizbullah, but next month it could be white supremacists or drug lords.

Once the others had left, Aaron Kurtzman lingered behind with John Kissinger, who was still seated at the conference table. Gesturing at the sketch on Kissinger's notepad, the Bear said, "Cough up, Cowboy. You've been acting spooked ever since I showed you the info on that popgun down in Birmingham. What did you mean when you said it was yours?"

"Long story," Kissinger murmured, crumpling the sketch in his fist and shooting the wad across the room. It bounced off the wall and into a wastebasket. Cowboy stood up. "Maybe I'll tell you about it sometime."

"I hope so, John." As they headed for the doorway, Kurtzman added, "If you want, I'll keep tabs on what's going on down there and let you know if there are any updates."

Kissinger managed a grateful half smile. "Thanks, Bear."

"My pleasure."

Kurtzman let himself into the communications room. Alone, Kissinger headed off in search of Brognola to apologize about daydreaming at the meeting and ask a question about the FOG-M. No matter how troubled he was over the possible implications of his old prototype turning up at a murder site in Alabama, he still had a job to do, and instead of mystery guns he turned his mind to the missile.

It wasn't easy.

3

Harlan Carruthers was an itinerant preacher, and his congregation was spread out along the back roads of Alabama. He spent most of his time roaming on foot, a Bible in one hand and a small dusty satchel with a few toiletry items in the other. Like his father before him, Harlan felt it his calling to bring the enlightenment of the Scriptures to those who might not otherwise have a chance at salvation. Often in his travels he would run across people who had no patience for the Gospel. He'd lost track of the times he'd been scorned, spat at, even beaten and robbed of the spare change that his more understanding listeners donated during the course of his roadside sermons. But, in keeping with the Lord's command, he always found it in his heart to forgive his enemies.

Until last month.

Last month, after fifteen long, grueling weeks on the road, searching for converts throughout the state, from the coastal shantytowns near Magnolia Springs to tiny border towns such as Shawmut, Hazel Green and Pickensville, Harlan started preaching his way toward the heartland and his hometown of Birmingham. He had a family waiting there for him. Carla and the two young kids, Everett and Charlotte. Lord, would it be good to see them again, he thought. When he'd called home on

Thanksgiving, Carla had said the children were growing like weeds, and that they wondered if their pa was coming home for Christmas. Of course he was.

Although Harlan mailed home what little money came his way, it was never enough to make ends meet for his family. To help stretch the budget Carla did ironing at their cramped trailer home outside the city limits, taking in loads from neighbors in the racially mixed trailer park. If possible she would try to fit in some baby-sitting while she ironed, figuring that keeping an eye on three or four children wasn't that much harder than looking after two. Somehow the bills had been paid, she'd told him on the phone, but with Christmas coming up it didn't look as if the Carrutherses would have a tree, much less any presents to put under it.

Harlan did his part, juggling his itinerary so that after Thanksgiving he was preaching in the more affluent regions of the state. He found a few places to preach where passersby gave him dimes and quarters instead of pennies and nickels. A couple of good Samaritans even tossed dollar bills into the faded black cap that he set on the ground near his feet whenever he stopped on a street corner or at the edge of a park to spread the Word.

A week before Christmas, he left Montgomery with almost sixty dollars in his pocket, an extravagant sum easily surpassing any previous monthly surplus he'd managed to set aside. His mind was filled with thoughts of the presents he could buy for his family. Lord knows they deserved something special for standing by him, a husband and father gone from their lives most of the year. It took a special kind of love to hold a family together under such circumstances, and Harlan gave thanks for all his blessings. Once he reached home, he would buy a new dress for Carla, toys and secondhand shoes for the children, then spend the rest of the sixty dollars on food for a proper Christmas dinner.

Halfway to Birmingham, Harlan Carruthers was jumped by a group of black teenagers out joyriding the back roads between Thorsby and Jemison. He pleaded for mercy but his words, like the prayers he recited feverishly even as fists were slamming into his midsection, fell on deaf ears. Battered and bruised, Harlan was left by the roadside in tattered clothes, his money and satchel stolen. All they had left him was his Bible. Normally a reserved, uncomplaining man in the eyes of his family, Harlan tearfully called home to tell Carla what had happened and to apologize that his plans for their Christmas had been shattered.

Carla tried to cheer her husband up, telling him that while rummaging through the trash Dumpsters behind the local market for day-old bread and produce items, she had come across a set of discarded Christmas tree lights. Equally providential, the neighbors in the trailer next door had mistakenly bought a dried-out Christmas tree and had tossed it out in favor of a newer one. Carla had taken the rejected tree into their trailer and strung it with the salvaged lights. She told Harlan that having him home for Christmas would be enough of a present for her and that she had a few dollars saved up that they could take to the Salvation Army to buy something for the kids. Harlan's tears of pain and shame turned to those of joy as he heard Carla say how much she loved him.

Hanging up the phone, Harlan dusted himself off and hiked straight to the nearest on-ramp for Highway 65, which would take him home. He couldn't wait to get there.

The trailer park was located south of Birmingham, on a small hill clustered with tall Southern pines, smaller dogwoods and bramble. The nearest highway exit was only a quarter mile away, and when Harlan stepped out of a station wagon and thanked the woman who had given him a ride all the way from Jemison, he could see a plume of black smoke rising from the park into the late-afternoon sky. Immediately concerned, Harlan cleared the distance to the park in long, loping strides, Bible clutched tightly against his chest as he whispered prayers all the way.

Again his prayers went unanswered.

The smoke was coming from his family's trailer. The park was in a state of chaos, with fire fighters and curiosity seekers getting in one another's way. Shouting his wife's name, Harlan wildly elbowed his way through the mob toward the fire. When he failed to spot Carla or either of the children in the crowd, he screamed and bolted toward the inferno.

"Carla! Everett! Charlotte!"

Before he could reach the flames, someone grabbed him from behind and pulled him clear of the fire fighters.

"Let me go!" Harlan glanced over his shoulder and saw that he was being held by Thurmond Cates, whose family lived in the trailer across from his own.

"It's too late," Thurmond shouted above the din.

"Let me go! My family's in there!" Try as he might, however, Harlan was no match for the other man's strength.

"I'm sorry, Preacher, but they're gone." Thurmond's eyes were red from more than the smoke.

"What?" Harlan's already pallid features turned even whiter. "No, you're lying!"

Thurmond shook his head sadly, easing up his grip on the preacher. "Nobody could get to them in time." He pointed over to an ambulance parked near the fire trucks. Three bodies were visible through the van's open doors, all of them covered.

Harlan stared at the ambulance for a long moment, oblivious to the snapping of flames and the shouted commands of fire fighters trying to bring the blaze under control. An eerie calm settled over him, and when he asked Thurmond a third time to let him go, the black man obliged. Walking over to where paramedics were just closing the doors on the ambulance, Carruthers identified himself and asked to see the bodies. One of the attendants reluctantly obliged and unzipped the thick plastic bags.

To Harlan's amazement, Carla, Everett and Charlotte all seemed to be slumbering peacefully, untouched by flame. The paramedic explained that they'd been asleep when the fire had started and had succumbed to smoke inhalation.

"How...?"

"The fire? They probably won't know for sure what started it for a while, but I heard them say something about faulty Christmas lights and the tree being too dry."

The attendant said something else, but Harlan was no longer listening. He thought back to his last conversation with Carla. She said she'd gotten the tree from the neighbors when they'd tossed it out.

The neighbors.

The Cateses.

Police were on the scene now, dispersing the crowd and giving the fire crews more room for mop-up. Harlan strode back to the smoldering remains of his home.

Gone. All gone.

Through all this Harlan had kept his Bible in one hand. It was an old Gideons, given to him by a hotel chamber-

maid in return for hearing her confession during one of
his wanderings. The pages were dog-eared from use, for
even though Preacher Carruthers knew countless pas-
sages by heart, he still relied upon the Good Book for
backup and support.

But not any longer.

Deep inside Harlan Carruthers, something snapped.

With an almost absentminded nonchalance, Harlan
tossed his Bible into a small fire at the edge of the trailer
remains. He watched flames eat at the frail pages and
eventually consume the entire book. Then he turned his
back on his home and his God.

Across the way, he saw the Cateses gathered in front of
their own, larger trailer, grimly looking on. Thurmond,
Vera, Uland, Jimmy, Lottie, Gram Cates—Harlan met
their gaze with his own, and in his eyes was a new and
terrifying emotion, an emotion he'd tried to deny all his
life and that now came over him with an overwhelming
force.

Hate...

But that was a month ago.

Now the Cateses were dead, all of them, and still Harlan Carruthers didn't feel fully avenged. What about the
people who ran that store and tossed the Christmas lights
into the Dumpster for Carla to find? Niggers. And the
gang that had jumped him on his way home, delaying
him crucial hours from reaching home? Niggers again.
He could go on and on, and he would always come to the
same conclusion: niggers everywhere were the cause for
the emptiness he felt. They should have to pay for what
had happened.

And they would.

For the past twelve hours Harlan had been thrashing
through the wilds, far from the roads where he had once

tried to win souls. Now he wanted to avoid everyone, except those he would seek out and meet on his own terms. He had another of the guns he'd come across that first night after the death of his family, when he'd sought refuge in liquor and had hatched the first mad dreams for revenge against those he held responsible for the misfortunes in his life. He still had only a faint recollection of how it had all happened. He remembered staggering out of a downtown bar after the first drinking binge he'd ever gone on and wandering aimlessly down side streets, unsure where his life would now take him. He'd stopped to relieve himself and had heard voices in the darkness of an alley. The rest was hazy. Some kind of argument. People shouting at him, approaching him from darkness. Him fighting back for the first time in his life, in a rage. Somehow getting his hand on a gun and firing it, then being alone, running crazily with a leather suitcase tucked under one arm, laughing at the moon.

He was too tired to laugh now. Tired, cold and hungry. His feet ached from the rough terrain he'd been fleeing across, and his clothes were soaked from the several creeks he'd slogged through in the night. There was a gray tinge of dawn to the east, and Harlan was wary of being in the open during daylight. He willed himself to clear the next rise, then paused to thank his new satanic allies for once again seeing to his needs, because just down the slope, nestled amid a stand of old conifers, was a small weathered cabin. Smoke curled up from a rusted tin chimney, promising warmth inside.

"Yes," he whispered to himself, taking a last deep breath before starting down the steep incline, careful to keep himself shielded from view of anyone who might happen to be looking out from the cabin. Thickets provided good cover but also snapped noisily when he ven-

tured too close to the brittle branches. He produced a pair
of light cotton gloves from his back pocket and put them
on before taking hold of his coveted semiautomatic pistol. The feel of the gun in his hand brought him a sense
of renewed strength and vigor. It made him feel in command, in control.

There was a small hand-painted sign posted farther up
the dirt road that linked the cabin to the rest of the world,
and in the predawn light Harlan saw that the sign adver-
tised Possums For Sale. As he stealthily approached the
cabin, the preacher noticed a number of the small beasts
housed in cages stacked together against a ramshackle
garage. Even from fifty yards away he could smell them,
and he wrinkled his nose with disgust at the unsavory
aroma.

The sound of an automobile grew disturbingly louder,
and before he could step up onto the wood-slat porch
leading to the cabin's front door, Carruthers was forced
to retreat quickly to the side of the house. Moments later
a pair of headlights cut a pale swath across the weed-
choked lawn and the front of the cabin. There was a
commotion inside the house, then a middle-aged black
woman stepped out onto the porch, wiping her hands on
an apron as she smiled at two men who got out of a decrepit Chevy pickup and circled around to lower the tail-
gate.

"Good catch?" the woman asked.

"Fine, real fine," the older of the two men boasted,
reaching over the bed of the pickup and patting a large
wire cage roughly the same size as those stacked near the
garage. Inside the cage were three full-grown possums.
As the men were preparing to unload their night's haul,
a huge baggy-faced hound howled from the front seat of

the vehicle and poked its head out the rolled-down window.

"Shaddup, Homer!" the younger of the men snapped at the mongrel. "You already met these varmints when you chased 'em up a tree, 'member?"

The hound continued to carry on, but its attention wasn't focused on the most recent additions to the possum farm, but rather the side of the cabin.

"Lordsakes!" the woman explained when she saw Harlan Carruthers step into view. She didn't notice his gun at first. "You half near scared me out of my skin, mister. What you doin' here about these parts this early, anyway?"

"Jessie Mae, get inside!" the older man commanded, letting go of the crate, which promptly tipped to one side and swung its door open, letting the possums free. He rushed to the front of the pickup, opening the door to let the hound out and to get at the shotgun rack mounted over the back seat.

No one heard the shots, but both men jerked off the sides of the truck and slumped to the dirt. Harlan swung his weapon around and fired two shots at Jessie Mae, who had been too stunned to follow the older man's orders. A red splotch appeared on her apron, matched by a bleeding wound where one of the 9 mm slugs tore through a buttonhole on her blouse. Reeling backward, she grabbed at the dangling chains of a hanging rocker for support. Harlan shot her one more time before taking aim at the bloodhound which barked loudly but refused to make a move toward the man with the gun. He pulled the trigger once, then again and again until the dog was silent.

Carruthers calmly checked the bodies to make sure that everyone was in fact dead, then he went into the cabin long enough to put together a picnic basket filled with food items and a couple of clear bottles of bootleg gin. He scooped a handful of steaming grits into a tin cup by the sink and set in a fork before taking the rations out to the Chevy.

Three more, he thought to himself proudly as he slipped in behind the steering wheel and started the engine. Four, if he counted the dog. Shifting into reverse, he turned the pickup around and headed off, back the same way the truck had come. He was pretty sure the road would eventually get him back to Birmingham.

As an afterthought, he waved his gun out the window and took a few potshots at crows perched on the power lines that supplied the cabin. The birds cawed loudly and flew off unharmed. When the gun was empty, Harlan let it drop to the side of the road. Once he got back to his hiding place, he'd still have one more gun left. He decided he'd try to learn how to reload that one.

4

"I dunno, it just doesn't seem like something up our alley," Carl Lyons said, staring down at Appalachian peaks that poked through the low clouds obscuring the borderland between Georgia and Alabama. He was sitting in one of the charter jets at the disposal of Stony Man operatives, sharing the primitive compartment with Schwarz, Blancanales and Kissinger.

"Of course it is," Pol countered. "You ask me, some wigged-out serial killer offing whole families is as much of a terrorist act as any Muslim fanatic doing his dirty business with a car bomb."

"Yeah, well, maybe you have a point," the Ironman conceded. He ran his hand along the part in his trimmed blond hair. His scalp was still itching from some irritation he'd picked up during an earlier assignment, and he suspected part of his foul disposition was due to the fact that Able Team had been shuttled onto the jet at a moment's notice before he'd had a chance to shower with his medicinal shampoo. Then, too, there was also that gnawing remnant of grief still tearing at him, putting him on edge. He was annoyed at his inability to shake off the doldrums and fall back on all the philosophical tenets that had always governed his life in the past.

Life is hard and then you die. You're all alone in this world. Just nut up and do it.

These were the creeds of self-reliant loners, and no one embodied those sayings more than Carl Lyons. But then why did he always end up trying to share his life with someone, only to have them die on him? Maybe it was a curse. The loner's curse. Fate telling him, Yes, Carl Lyons, in the end you will always be alone.

"Shit," he sighed, trying to throw off his gloom and pick up the conversation.

"Besides," Schwarz was saying, "this whole thing about the murder weapons bears looking into just on its own. Right, Cowboy?"

Kissinger nodded. When Kurtzman had come to him with news of another mass murder outside Birmingham that involved an almost identical copy of the mystery gun used in the first slayings, Cowboy had come forward with his concern that somehow his supposedly long-lost QA-18 semiautomatic had resurfaced. The others had listened with interest, and not only because Kissinger had previously avoided any mention of his ill-fated venture in Wisconsin. Hal Brognola had been the first to think a few steps ahead and guess at the possible implications. Now, in the jet, Kissinger reiterated his superior's thinking.

"The QA-18 was naturally intended for use by our side," he explained, passing around photocopies of the gun that Kurtzman had gleaned off his computers and the wire services. "But, unfortunately, it would also make for an ideal terrorist weapon.

"I designed the gun so that it would require minimum maintenance and minimum parts, which translates into low-cost manufacture. Put that together with the fact that it has a built-in silencer, flash suppressor and fifteen-shot ammo cartridge and you've got a perfect weapon for the kind of mass killing where you'd want to maintain an element of surprise."

Blancanales chanced a metaphor. "You mean it'll fire on rock and roll without anyone hearing the drums."

"Something like that," Kissinger said. "If these things are being mass-produced illegally somewhere and end up in the wrong hands, we could find ourselves up against an army that can make a night raid and gun down people in their sleep without making any more noise than a swarm of mosquitoes."

"You've obviously never heard mosquitoes in Mexico, *amigo*," Pol cracked. "Down there they sound like chain saws."

Lyons took a closer look at the photo. "And you're sure this is based on your designs?"

"I can't be positive until I hold it in my hands," Kissinger admitted. "But the similarities are just too close for coincidence."

"Strange," Gadgets reflected. "I mean, if your partner got crisped along with all the plans and prototypes in that fire you told us about—"

"Yeah, I know it doesn't add up," Cowboy cut in. "That's why I've been so damn antsy since I first heard about it. There's got to be an explanation, and I can't wait to get to the bottom of it."

"Won't be much longer," Lyons noted, seeing wide bends of the Coosa River appear through a gap in the thinning cloud cover.

"Well, we're with you all the way on this, Cowboy," Blancanales pledged to the weaponsmith. "After all the help you've thrown our way since taking over for Konzaki, we owe you."

"I appreciate it, guys."

"Of course, we're under orders, too," Schwarz said with a grin, "so don't get too teary-eyed with gratitude."

The men laughed, then slapped on their seat belts as the jet began its descent toward Birmingham.

"You know, maybe we oughta form a union and demand better working conditions, eh? Missions should be regulated with a month off between each," Blancanales suggested.

"Yeah, right," Schwarz said. "Maybe we should get Brognola to bring it up the next time he visits Congress. Have 'em pass a resolution that terrorists can't put in more than a forty-hour week."

"If they tried that, you can be sure the terrorists would hire the ACLU to fight it," Lyons drawled cynically. "And we all know who'd win then."

"The lawyers on both sides," Blancanales said.

Lyons nodded. "I guess on second thought we'll just stick to our way of doing things...."

5

Red Mountain jutted upward along the southern perimeter of Birmingham, its timbered ridge providing a clear view of the city below. Motorists driving along the section of Highway 31 that cut through the rising slope could see vast strips of the exposed red ore that had given the mountain its name. They could also, at some point, catch a glimpse of the landscaped fifteen-acre park that crowned the uppermost peak.

In the center of that park, standing atop a 120-foot-high stone pedestal, was the largest iron statue in the world, a fifty-five-foot-tall, sixty-ton likeness of Vulcan, mythological god of fire and the forge. It was an appropriate mascot for a city that had experienced its initial boom based on industry that had grown from the region's vast supply of iron ore. It had been raw ore from Red Mountain that had been transported to Selma during the Civil War for transformation into cannons and shot used by the Confederate army.

Vulcan stood next to a massive anvil, and held a blacksmith's hammer in one brawny hand. His other arm was held upright, brandishing a torch that he stared at with a look of bold intensity. Traditionally a red light built into the torch was turned on as a memorial gesture whenever the city experienced a traffic fatality. Today, however, the torch was lit in memory of the second family of victims gunned down by the unknown assassin who had instilled an epidemic of fear unmatched in the South since the Green River slayings of the previous decade.

The assassin stood on the ground beneath the statue of Vulcan, sharing the view of Birmingham. Across the valley where the city sprawled, smokestacks intruded upon the horizon like massive fence posts. For years the chimneys had spewed factory by-products into the air, creating dire smog problems that had eventually led to the strictest environmental controls in the area. Most of the stacks, and some of the factories themselves, were abandoned ruins, and it was in one of the buildings that Harlan Carruthers had initially hid his supply of stolen handguns. He'd been there earlier in the day, comparing the last of the weapons with diagrams in a book on gun handling he'd picked up at the library after cleaning up and changing into a newly acquired set of clothes. The pistol was tucked inside the waistband of his pants, hidden from view by his black jacket. Now Harlan knew how to reload it with the ammunition he'd found in the same case as the guns. By his count he still had nearly two thousand rounds of 9 mm bullets, more than enough to seek out and eliminate his avowed enemies.

Tiring of the view, Harlan picked up his satchel and went over to buy the late edition of the *Birmingham Daily* from a vending machine set near the entrance to a geological museum situated inside the base of the statue. He took the paper to a bench at the edge of the park and felt a warm arousal in his loins as he carefully read over the half-dozen in-depth stories relating to the unsolved murders. There were photos of the victims as well as of the murder sites, and the preacher reveled in the rush of fresh memories they triggered. What a glorious mission he was on. Particularly invigorating was Harlan's revelation that although the authorities had the weapons used in the killings, they had no other clues and were pleading with the public to come forward with any information that might help their investigation.

The public wouldn't be able to help, Carruthers mused as he turned the pages. His cause was backed by higher forces than those of mere men, and until he achieved his destiny no one would be able to stop him. He felt, despite his cloying fatigue, a sense of invincibility that was overmatched by an even more powerful urge.

To kill again.

He set the paper down and looked around him. Most of the people at the park were congregated around the huge statue, but there were a few families enjoying themselves in the grassy clearings set between scattered trees. He toyed with the idea of going up to the observatory platform located just beneath the statue and cutting loose with the gun, just to see how many people he could kill in one outing. It was a strong temptation that he ultimately resisted, feeling it was better to assure his anonymity. By choosing his killing grounds more carefully, the death toll would rise quickly enough. Better to play it slow and savor each incident. Besides, he reasoned, there were more than just niggers about, and he didn't want to blaspheme his mission by killing whites.

From Vulcan Park it was only a short walk to another of the main tourist attractions in Birmingham, the Botanical Gardens. Spread out over sixty-seven acres, the park boasted myriad varieties of flowers, both those indigenous to the area and those transplanted from other regions and countries. Harlan paid a token admission fee and wandered down the winding dirt paths, working his way deeper into the park. He passed the Touch and See garden for the blind and the large floral park with its floral clock that reminded him less than twenty-four hours had passed since he had gunned down the Cates family on the Cahaba River only a few miles away. He couldn't believe it. Only that long ago? It seemed like an eternity.

After walking through the park for nearly an hour, Harlan finally came across the ideal setting he'd been looking for—the Japanese Garden, an area adjacent to the main park devoted to the flowers and landscaping of the Orient. Off by themselves, a black family of four was gathered near a high-arched bridge that spanned a narrow brook filled with bright red koi fish. The father was off to one side, peering through the viewfinder of his mounted camera as he tried to herd his wife and kids into the frame with the bridge in the background.

"If you want, I'd be glad to take the picture so you can be in it, too," Harlan offered casually as he sauntered over.

"Would you?" the father said, stepping away from the tripod. "That would be great!"

Harlan watched patiently as the other man briefed him on how to use the camera. As the father walked over to join his family, the preacher unzipped his jacket but still kept the pistol hidden from view. He glanced through the viewfinder. This was going to be great. The media would have a field day with what he was about to offer them.

"Okay," he told the family, discreetly letting his right hand slip inside his jacket and secure a grip on the pistol. "Everybody smile!"

"You heard the man," the father prompted, checking to make sure the others were taking their cues. When he glanced back at the camera, his own smile promptly dissolved and his jaw hung open.

Harlan shot the father first, taking a snapshot as the man's legs gave out beneath him and he keeled backward into the brook. Advancing the film with his left hand, the preacher shifted his gun slightly to the right and fired a few quick bursts at the wife as the camera documented the silencing of her screams. The children went down last, a bullet apiece drilled into their small bodies. The youngest had been only two years old, barely old enough to take a frail step before falling across the inert form of her mother.

Harlan stood up slowly and backed away from the camera, gun still in his hand. He pitied the poor newspaper editors throughout the nation who would have to decide which of the photographs would be best for the front page of tomorrow's papers. It sure wouldn't be an easy choice. He'd given them so much to choose from.

"Hey, you!" a voice cut through the silence behind him. "What the hell's going on here?"

A park official, wearing a khaki uniform, was approaching Harlan in a three-wheeled service cart. She hadn't seen the bodies lying near the bridge, but when she spotted the gun in Harlan's hand, she grabbed a microphone from the cart's dashboard and started to call out an alarm.

"Oh, no you don't," Harlan told her, squeezing off three shots at the woman. She dropped the microphone and sagged clear of the vehicle. An urgent voice sounded over the small speaker of the dash radio, asking for more information. Carruthers rushed over and set the microphone back in its cradle.

He looked down at the woman, stunned. She was white. How could it be? He could have sworn her skin was black. He'd stepped beyond his calling. This was wrong. All wrong. He had to get away, to think this all through. Help me, Satan, he cried out with his inner voice. Guide me. Forgive me.

The preacher slipped into the driver's seat and guided the cart away from the murder scene. His mind was still racing, cut loose like a mad dog off its tether. He frantically veered down a side path and was cutting through a groomed patch of vibrant camelias when he spotted a park truck heading his way.

The other vehicle was decidedly faster than the cart, and although the smaller size gave Harlan greater maneuverability, he knew that he could only elude the truck for a short time before he would be overtaken. Worse yet, he was now driving into a more frequented part of the gardens and was slowed down when strolling tourists failed to give him the right of way on the paths until he was on the verge of running them over. Other park officials had also joined in on the chase, keeping their distance when he fired wildly in their direction and yet gradually closing in on him.

As he approached the outer fringe of the park, Harlan finally abandoned the cart and vaulted over a fence that led down a steep incline to a highway spur that separated the gardens from Birmingham Zoo, one of the South's largest municipal collections of exotic beasts.

Traffic was heavy enough to prevent Harlan from crossing the tarmac at first, but once he leveled his weapon and shot a driver in the lane closest to him, the resulting chain reaction of accidents put all lanes out of commission. Now in a maddened frenzy, with no thoughts of grand missions but rather of flight, the preacher fired indiscriminately in his desperate charge across the roadway.

Reaching the zoo grounds, Harlan paused to catch his breath and quickly reload the weapon. His practice back at the hideout paid off. In a matter of seconds he was forcing his way past a stunned security guard, blowing out the man's brains when he tried to prevent the preacher from turning himself loose on the thousands of patrons who erroneously believed that the deadliest animals were safely behind bars.

6

The jet carrying Able Team touched down at Birmingham Municipal Airport and jockeyed away from the main terminals to a remote hangar where two marked police cruisers and a plain sedan were parked. It was a precautionary procedure, due to the secretive nature of any mission that involved Able Team, and also because the three-man army traveled with enough munitions to give permanent nightmares to any conscientious airport security team. Besides the customary retooled .45s and M-16s, the trio's "luggage" contained one Colt Python, one Atchisson shotgun, one standard Barrett M-82, two designer Uzis and an assortment of flash grenades, incendiary devices and other implements of the anti-terrorist trade.

A ground crew rolled out the mobile staircase and maneuvered it into place as the door to the jet's passenger compartment swung open. Lyons, the group's unofficial leader, was first out, turning up the collar of his jacket against a brisk gust of wind that blew across the airstrip. He was followed by Blancanales and Schwarz, with Kissinger bringing up the rear. As they proceeded down the steps, the welcoming committee materialized from out of the parked cars. Four cops and a man in a suit that reeked of the Bureau.

"Ross Coe, FBI," the latter introduced himself to Lyons, speaking with a faint drawl in his gravelly voice. He was a squat, thick-chested man with a round face and a bushy mustache that contained more hair than his balding scalp.

Lyons shook the man's hand, and quick introductions were exchanged as Kissinger and Able Team joined the others on terra firma. As they headed for the parked vehicles, Schwarz asked, "Anything new?"

Coe shook his head. "We were hoping that ballistics would have turned up a lead on the manufacturer, but no such luck."

The squawk box in one of the cruisers came to life, and two of the officers excused themselves to respond to the call. The others went over to the unmarked sedan, where Coe opened the trunk and removed a pair of matching pistols in clear plastic bags. "Which one of you's the expert?"

Kissinger stepped forward and took one of the wrapped weapons. His pulse once again kicked into overdrive as he looked the gun over. There could be no mistaking it now. He turned his head and nodded tersely at Lyons.

"Recognize it?" Coe asked Kissinger.

"Yeah, but I don't have any leads on it if that's what you're after."

Coe looked miffed. "I thought that's what the hoopla about you coming out here was all about."

"You thought wrong," Kissinger replied.

One of the officers who had checked on the radio call shouted over the roof of his car, "He's been spotted out at the zoo."

"What?" Coe blurted.

"Gone way off the deep end from the sound of it," the cop went on. "They say he's killed at least five more and wounded another dozen and is still going strong."

"Let's get going!" Lyons snapped, taking charge. Fortunately Brognola had greased the skids prior to Able Team's arrival, and the local authorities knew that the Ironman's commands had top priority.

As the three cars were started, Schwarz and Blancanales raided the luggage that had just been unloaded from the jet, breaking out the M-16s and the .45 revolvers. Lyons took his share of the ordnance and slipped into one of the patrol cars. Schwarz got in the second cruiser while Kissinger and Blancanales rode with Coe.

"Who the fuck are you guys, anyway?" the cop in the lead car asked Lyons as they hauled ass out of the airport and sirened their way onto the nearest thoroughfare.

"We ain't the damn Boy Scouts, I'll tell you that much," Lyons replied from the back seat as he clamped an ammo clip into the breach of his M-16.

The driver rolled down his window and spat out a brown stream of tobacco juice. Unlike the stereotype Southern lawman, he was lean in frame but baby-faced, looking more like Walter Mitty indulging in one of his private fantasies. His name was Donnie Welch. He cast a sidelong glance at his burly partner and sniggered. "Kind of a shame this loonie had to show himself so soon, eh?"

"How's that, Donnie?" the man riding shotgun asked. "Hell, we might have a chance to bag him and get our mugs in the papers."

"That's true, I 'spose, but he was doin' such a fine job of weedin' out niggers, I figured we'd give him a few more weeks before we took him off target practice...."

Donnie's partner chortled, but Lyons was silent except for the creak of the seat springs as he sat forward and regarded the men in front of him. "I don't know about you assholes," he said with a menacing calm, "but I put in a few years sharing my beat with some brothers in L.A., and there were more than a couple of times they put their necks on the line to keep me from ending up laid out in a box."

The second officer blushed slightly at Lyons's retort, but Welch rolled his eyes and clucked his tongue. "Whaddya know, a bleeding heart that packs a piece. Never thought I'd live to see that."

"Tell you what, shit-for-brains," Lyons taunted. "Let's take care of business here, then maybe later you and I can get together and talk politics."

Donnie glared at Lyons in the rearview mirror. "You got yourself a deal, blondie. Better yet, why don't you bring along the kraut and the spic so's we can play United Nations?"

Lyons eased back in his seat, trying to keep his temper at bay. It really grilled his goose that it only took a handful of morons like those in the front seat to soil the reputations of any given law-enforcement agency. Go through the ranks of any police or federal force, and for every nine guys that were in uniform because they felt a true desire to uphold the law, you'd find one closet fascist who looked on his badge as a license to wreak hell on anyone whose skin or accent was different than his own. Lyons had experienced it during his years with the LAPD, and it was one of the reasons he was glad he'd quit the unit in favor of Able Team.

They rode the rest of the way in silence, leading the other two cars through the snarl of traffic surrounding the zoo. An all-points bulletin had been issued, and it seemed as if half the Birmingham police force was already crowded into the parking lot by the time Able Team showed up with their local contingent. A quarter of the force's manpower was tied up in handling traffic and another third was busy dealing with the hysterical crowds that had been caught in the gunfire. Two choppers with highway patrol insignias were hovering above the zoo, banking periodically for closer looks at various exhibits and outbuildings. There were additional sirens wailing from paramedic vans taking casualties to the nearby University of Alabama Medical Center, one of the most reputable hospitals in the world. Other ambulances proceeded at a less frantic pace to the city morgue.

Kissinger joined Able Team in a huddle with the officer in command at the scene, a hulking captain named Durango who looked as if he moonlighted as Frankenstein's monster.

"He stopped firing a few minutes ago over near the monkey house," Durango reported, pointing out locations on a directory of the zoo grounds posted near where he'd parked his car. "We've got the area surrounded, but he won't show himself."

Lyons surveyed the layout and plotted his group's plan of attack. "Have your men hold their positions," he told the captain. "We'll come up around either side of them and branch out in case he managed to slip through."

"Fair enough." Durango fingered a walkie-talkie and relayed the instructions while Able Team split up. Lyons teamed with Schwarz while Kissinger headed off in the other direction with Blancanales. Several other local officers, including Donnie and his hefty sidekick, fanned out even farther from the route to the monkey house.

"I rode out here with a couple Cro-Magnons," Lyons told Schwarz as they ran, side by side, past caged exhibits where a variety of birds filled the air with a cacophony of chirps and shrill cries. "Talked like their daddies were the ones that let attack dogs loose on demonstrators back in the sixties."

"Some things never change, I guess," Schwarz muttered.

"It's bad enough having scum for an enemy."

When they reached an intersection of footpaths Lyons checked the signpost to make sure they were headed in the right direction, then led his partner past a pen filled with gazelles and other antelopes. Both men fell quiet and turned their concentration on the surrounding foliage and rock formations. The zoo was a veritable sniper's paradise with all the natural cover it provided, and each time there was a shifting shadow or rustling in the trees, Lyons or Schwarz would reflexively jerk to one side and swing his M-16 into play. More often than not, the motion they detected was caused by the stiff breeze, but twice the men had to hold back on the trigger when they spotted an armed figure they'd quickly recognized as Birmingham's equivalent of a SWAT member.

"Good thing Durango let them know we were coming or we'd be Swiss cheese by now," Schwarz told Lyons.

"Right," the Ironman agreed. "But we better stick close together just to be safe."

A few hundred yards away, Blancanales and Kissinger were making their way past the elephant display. A pair of wrinkled pachyderms watched them with tiny eyes.

"I wish I had their skin right now," Pol whispered. "I tell you, *amigo*, if I'd known we were going to be jumping into the frying pan as soon as we got off the plane, I'd have put on the Teflon undies."

"Amen to that," Kissinger said. "I don't like the idea that ... whoah, just a minute ..."

Cowboy stopped and crouched over the concrete walkway, picking something off the ground.

"¿Qué pasa?" Pol inquired, peering over Kissinger's shoulder.

"Well, we're on the right track," the weaponsmith said, holding out a spent bullet casing for Pol to see. Unlike the conventionally rounded variety, this cartridge was triangular. "When I bumped the ammo clip up to fifteen rounds, I took a cue from the old .38 Dardricks," he explained. "More efficient storage capacity."

"Then our man's been through here, eh?"

Kissinger nodded and sniffed the cartridge before slipping it into his pocket. He was about to rise from his crouch when he noted a glint of light off to his right. Instinctively he lunged to one side, tackling Pol to the ground just as a gunshot buzzed past the spot he'd just vacated. A second bullet clanged noisily off a trash bin behind Blancanales.

"Gracias, amigo," Pol said after he and Kissinger had scrambled to cover behind an abandoned vending cart. "Not bad for a wide receiver."

Peering in the direction the shots had come from, Cowboy saw a man dressed in black flee into the brush behind an enclosure for the zoo's giraffes. "Let's go!" he cried, breaking cover and taking up the chase.

HARLAN CARRUTHERS RAN like the possessed man that he was. A sprawl of rugged terrain between exhibits made for hard going, and he winced with pain when he turned his ankle while ducking behind a clump of dogwoods to avoid detection by the police chopper hovering overhead.

"We have you surrounded!" a voice boomed down at him from the helicopter, resonating through a hand-held bullhorn. "Throw down your weapon and come out into the open with your hands above your head!"

There was no way Harlan was going to surrender. Wiping sweat from his brow with his right shirtsleeve, he peered up through the leafy branches and could clearly see the chopper, dangling in the air less than thirty yards from him. A sharpshooter was poised in the aircraft's open doorway, scanning the grounds below through his rifle's scope. It would only be a matter of seconds before Harlan fell into the weapon's sights.

"Guide my aim," he implored Satan, raising his automatic pistol and drawing a bead on the gunman in the copter. He pulled the trigger repeatedly until the sharpshooter dropped his rifle and plummeted through the treetops, snapping branches loudly before landing in the brush less than twenty feet away from Harlan. The preacher had little time to gloat over his realization that the dead man's skin was black, because seconds later there was a massive explosion and the ground around him shook as the helicopter itself crashed into the rocks near the giraffe quarters. Fire and smoke gushed forth from the debris, spreading to the nearby brush. Pushed along by the substantial crosswinds, the blaze spread toward Harlan.

"No!"

The preacher turned and bolted in the opposite direction, fleeing recklessly, no longer mindful of the dangers around him. He broke clear of the brush and began scrambling over a cluster of boulders, only to lose his footing and slip down a steep embankment. The gun fell clear of his hand and clattered beyond reach as he came to rest on level ground. Shaken by the fall, it was several moments before the man came fully back to his senses and was able to place the disturbing sound behind him. He slowly turned around, blood streaming from a gash on his cheek, and froze with fear.

From out of the shadows of a man-made cave, a full-grown African lion appeared, baring powerful fangs as it growled loudly at the prey that had fallen into its cage.

LYONS AND SCHWARZ WERE close by when the helicopter crashed. Gingerly scaling the craggy shell surrounding the giraffe exhibit, they tried to get to the wreckage but were repelled by the intense heat of the fire. It was painfully obvious that there could be no survivors. Smoke stung their eyes as they circled around the course of the brushfire and resumed their search for the man responsible for the deadly inferno.

"Over there!" Schwarz cried out, spotting Harlan lose his balance and fall from view into the lion's den. Lyons and Gadgets sprinted in pursuit, M-16s at the ready in case the killer's fall had been a ruse meant to fool his pursuers into dropping their guard.

Two other lions had crept out from their inside quarters by the time Gadgets and Lyons reached the south perimeter of the carnivores' den. Pol and Kissinger had just arrived from the other direction and stood near a railing fifty yards away. All four men stared down at the pathetic figure of Harlan Carruthers, who was on his knees like a Christian about to be martyred in the Colosseum.

"You're not getting off that easy," Gadgets said, starting down the same incline Harlan had cleared with considerably less finesse. Over his shoulder he shouted at Lyons, "Tell those lions I'm not coming down for lunch."

The Ironman rattled off a burst from his M-16, raising dirt in front of the snarling lions and driving them back. Blancanales went one step farther, clearing the railing and leaping down into the opposite end of the pit from where Gadgets was attempting to rescue the preacher.

"Over here," Pol cried out to the lions, waving his free arm to get their attention while he kept his M-16 ready with the other. As he edged his way carefully toward the opening that led back to their indoor cages, he called out to Gadgets. "Okay, get him out of here!"

All three of the lions started for Blancanales, turning their backs on Schwarz and the disarmed assassin. Gadgets roughly jerked Carruthers to his feet and dragged him to the edge of the pit. Without his gun and his dreams of grandeur, Harlan was no longer the invincible right arm of Satan but rather a scrawny, trembling figure who mutely complied with Gadgets's orders that he reach up and take hold of the hand Lyons was extending down to him from atop the stone ledge.

As the Ironman hauled the preacher up, Kissinger took over covering Blancanales from the other side of the den's outlying boundary.

"Careful, Pol," he called down to the wiry man in the pit.

"Don't worry, I will," Blancanales shouted back as he reached the opened steel-barred gate next to the cave entrance. To get there he had to step out of Kissinger's view and leave himself uncovered except for his own weapon, which at best might be able to stop one or two of the beasts should they decide it was feeding time.

There was a momentary standoff as the lions held their ground, still eyeing Blancanales and growling with sure menace through their wide, lethal jaws. Behind the beasts, Pol could see Gadgets following the killer up to safe ground.

"Well, kitties, it's down to just you and me," he told the creatures as he pointed his M-16 skyward and stepped behind the gate. "Nap time..."

All three of the beasts tensed on their formidable haunches as if preparing to lunge forward. Less than ten feet separated Pol from nearly two tons of man-eating fury when he fired his rifle in the air just above the lions' bushy manes. As he had hoped, the proximity of the cave entrance wasn't lost on the creatures when they reacted to the thundering blasts of the M-16. Charging past Blancanales, they sought refuge in the dark interior and disappeared from view. Pol hurriedly closed the gate behind them and slapped the safety latch into place. When one of the lions doubled back, steel bars prevented it from getting at the man who had trespassed into their lair.

"My, what big teeth you have, Grandma," Blancanales wisecracked, backing away from the cave entrance until he was back in Kissinger's sights.

"You ought to get in touch with Ringling Brothers," Cowboy told Pol as he helped the shorter man out of the exhibit.

"No big deal," Blancanales scoffed, dusting himself off. "I mean, who ever heard of lions eating out Mexican?"

The two men walked over to where Lyons and Schwarz were already interrogating their prisoner. A broken man, Harlan was offering no resistance.

"You can spill your guts about everything else later," Lyons barked at Carruthers, holding out the QA-18 Gadgets had retrieved from the spot where Harlan had dropped it. "But right now you better tell us how you got your hands on this gun."

"I . . . I can't remember," Harlan stammered. "I was drunk and—"

"Think!" Lyons shouted, jerking the man over to the railing and turning his head so that he faced down into the lion's den. All three of the creatures were clamoring near the gateway. "Or maybe you want to go back and try your luck down there?"

Harlan's eyes bugged, and he shook his head wildly. "No. I'll try to remember." Flustered, he sorted through the shorted circuitry of his brain for some recollection of that night a week ago. "It was late at night. I—I was in a back alley . . . somewhere downtown . . . all that drinking, I had to answer nature's call. You see, I went to a bar. . . . I think it was near the highway. . . . I don't normally drink, but that night was different because—"

"Spare us the fucking miniseries!" Lyons shook Harlan fiercely, shoving him halfway over the railing. "Just tell us who you got the goddamn guns from!"

"Help!" Carruthers flailed his arms like a spastic bird.

Pol placed a hand on Lyons's shoulder, and the two men exchanged glances. Both knew the next course of action. Routine interrogation tactics. Whack 'em with the right hand, stroke 'em with the left.

"Okay, okay, *amigo*," Blancanales told Lyons, pulling the Ironman away from Harlan. "Give the man a little space, eh?"

"Screw it!" Lyons raged, though he winked at Pol when Harlan wasn't looking. "I say we drag him over to that chopper he shot down and roast his pale little ass on the flames till he talks."

"Chill out, Ironman," Gadgets said, playing his role in the charade.

"Okay, fella," Pol told Harlan, a trace of friendliness in his voice. "We know you're trying to cooperate, so let's take it nice and slow. You said you were drunk and out in some alley taking a leak, right?"

Harlan nodded, shamefaced. "Yes. Like I said, I'm not a drinking man by nature, so after spending all night at the bar—" He rolled his eyes upward, trying to remember the place's name. "It was the Bull Bar, something like that."

"That's okay. We don't need to go into all that right now," Pol told him. "While you were in the alley, what happened? You heard someone? Saw something?"

"Yes," Harlan murmured. "Men. Three of them, I think. When they heard me, they stopped talking. I don't remember what they said, but they called me some kind of name and came after me. I was in a bad mood, and with all the booze."

Kissinger joined in the interrogation. "Tell us more about the men. Did you get a good look at any of them?"

"It was dark," Harlan recalled. "Everything happened so fast.

"Think," Cowboy prompted. "It's important."

Harlan was silent a moment, then a spark of recollection lit his eyes. "One of the men . . . I took the gun from him. Yes, I remember, he had red hair, and his nose looked like it was broken." The preacher took a tentative step away from the railing, lost in thought. "And another guy was real tall and had a—"

A distant gunshot echoed across the zoo grounds.

Harlan Carruthers's confession was over. Blood bubbled up through his thin lips and life fled his eyes as he crumpled to the ground. A neat hole in the back of his coat marked the spot where the bullet had entered, shearing his spine en route to his heart.

"What the . . . !"

Lyons whirled around. He'd been on the visiting end of sniper fire enough times to be able to gauge the trajectory of a shot. So had the rest of Able Team, and they all had their eyes on the baby-faced officer who'd driven Lyons to the zoo.

Donnie Welch stepped clear of a picnic bench thirty yards away and holstered his service revolver. "Bastard was about to make a run for it," he told the men gathered around Harlan's body.

"Like hell he was," Lyons retorted. "You knew your orders. He was ours."

Donnie shrugged his shoulders. "What can I say? It was a judgment call."

The remaining helicopter swung into view overhead, and the other law-enforcement officers began to converge near the lion exhibit. Pol knelt over Harlan long enough to confirm the man was indeed dead.

"Besides," Welch went on, "the way I see it, we just saved the taxpayers a bundle, right? No long fucking trial and legal hocus-pocus to bother with." He glanced down at the body. "Fucker's right where he belongs."

"Maybe so," Lyons conceded, "but you took him out before he could give us a few answers we were looking for."

"I didn't see his lawyer anywhere," Donnie defended himself. "You couldn't have used anything he told you, so what's the problem?"

"You're the problem, chubface," Lyons said.

Before the standoff could escalate any further, Captain Durango arrived on the scene and took charge of the men under his command. Welch walked away from Able Team but managed to turn back long enough to give

Lyons and the others a view of his middle finger. "Take a twirl on this," he said to them.

Lyons took a step in Donnie's direction, but Pol placed a hand on his shoulder. "Let him go, Ironman. He's not worth the aggravation."

Lyons reluctantly backed off and joined his comrades in walking away from the exhibit. Schwarz gave the QA-18 to Kissinger and apologized, saying, "Sorry we came up with a dead end, Cowboy."

"No dead end," Kissinger mumbled, and for the first time the others noticed how distraught the weaponsmith looked.

"What do you mean?" Pol asked.

"My partner back in Wisconsin had red hair and a pug nose," Kissinger replied.

"Crosley?" Lyons frowned. "I thought he was dead."

Kissinger stared hard at the weapon he thought he would never see again. "So did I."

7

The man who had died in Howie Crosley's place during that fateful Wisconsin chemical fire had been a low-life drifter by the name of Kent Rembo. Crosley had met the transient several weeks before the blaze at a disreputable strip bar on the outskirts of Madison, near the train tracks that had brought Rembo to town. The men had talked away the evening over several pitchers of beer, with Rembo under the mistaken notion that Crosley had been to Nam the same time he'd been grunting his way through a four-year hitch with the marines.

After closing time, Howie further befriended the stranger, not only arranging for him to receive a new set of clothes and free boarding at a run-down flophouse Howie owned in nearby Verona, but also seeing to it that Rembo received dental care for his long-untended teeth. In exchange for Crosley's generosity, the drifter had only to stay put at the boardinghouse and perform a few menial tasks during the day. It was the kind of offer a loser like Rembo was more than happy to accept.

The man who performed the work on Rembo's teeth was also Crosley's regular dentist, and when the doctor left the country for an extended vacation in Europe, Crosley had little difficulty in breaking into his office and switching Rembo's dental charts with his own.

Two days later, in response to an urgent call from Crosley, Rembo checked out of the boardinghouse and took a bus from Verona to a Holiday Inn located down the road from the office building where both Crosley and John Kissinger worked. Following Crosley's instructions, Rembo checked into the hotel for one night, paying in advance and telling the manager he had to leave early the following day. He got up at five in the morning and walked to the office building, again heeding Howie's advice to remain as inconspicuous as possible as he waited near the side entrance to the building.

Howie came downstairs from his second-story office just as dawn was breaking over Madison. He let Rembo inside and offered him some coffee he'd supposedly just bought from a vending machine in the side hallway. After taking several sips of the coffee, Kent Rembo slumped to the floor in a drugged stupor. Crosley dragged the body into the nearby stairwell, then backtracked to the side hallway, pausing near the entrance to the chemical supply storeroom long enough to tamper with the power box and wiring, thereby starting the fire that would soon after destroy the entire building, all of its contents and char the bodies of its victims so drastically that dental records would have to be consulted to make positive identification.

But Crosley didn't walk away from his life and identity in Madison empty-handed. He'd made copies of John Kissinger's designs for the QA-18, and he fled south with the plans, along with three hundred thousand dollars in cash he was supposed to have turned over to a Switzerland-bound Mafia courier in the last of a long series of laundering schemes he'd been involved with on behalf of the Wisconsin mob in recent years. Organized crime had been Howie Crosley's secret mistress and the real source of most of the income he'd attributed to his engineering and real estate ventures. He'd strung along Kissinger in the belief that there was a considerable fortune to be made by peddling a weapon like the QA-18 to the mob, but the closer the weapon had come to being a reality, the less Crosley had wanted to share the profits he envisioned coming from its manufacture.

The fire was intended to serve several purposes. Besides taking Kissinger out of the picture, by faking his death Crosley figured to avoid his own demise at the hands of the Wisconsin Mafia once they realized their most recent laundering of funds hadn't taken place as scheduled.

Crosley fled south to Alabama, where he laid low for several years, living off the stolen funds while he created a new identity for himself and personally slaved over Kissinger's designs for the QA-18 until he came up with the final adjustments and put together a new prototype.

Now, around Birmingham, Crosley was known as Evan Grossler, and although the manufacturing plant he owned in the city's congested industrial sector primarily concerned itself with the production of spare parts for lawn mowers and snowmobiles, there was a clandestine back room where a trial run of ten QA-18s were turned out for use in demonstrations for potential customers. Crosley was sure he'd done a more than adequate job of covering tracks with regards to his Wisconsin roots, but when it had come time to market his weapon, rechristened the Stealthshooter, he was determined to steer clear of sales pitches to Alabama's organized crime syndicate. The way he saw it, there were plenty of other groups he could do business with without running the risk of having his past come back to haunt him.

And he was right.

Between survivalist networks, right-wing paramilitary groups, the Ku Klux Klan and a wide range of other radical organizations Crosley had made contact with during his years in Birmingham, he had a long enough list of prospective clients to ensure the fortune he always knew the Stealthshooter was capable of bringing him. He'd put the pistol into full production in anticipation of windfall profits once the gun hit the black market.

And then had come the run of bad luck.

First there had been the rendezvous with the local Grand Dragon of the Ku Klux Klan and one of his key henchmen. They'd met one night in a back alley near Crosley's manufacturing plant. He'd brought along a display suitcase with three of the weapons and more than two thousand rounds of ammunition. The plan had been for them to ride out to the country so that the Klansmen could sample each of the weapons and assure themselves that they were reliable enough to be added to their organization's arsenal.

However, within moments after making contact in the alley, the men had been surprised by some deranged vagrant who was oblivious to their warnings that he find another place to piss. A fight had broken out, and the stranger had somehow managed to claw his way free of the other two men and run off with the sample Stealthshooters after nearly gunning Crosley down with one of them. Fortunately Crosley had had backup pistols to show the Grand Dragon, and a tentative deal had been struck.

Then had come the headlines about mystery weapons being involved in the mass murder of two local black families. Although in a way the news was a form of free advertisement for the gun's effectiveness, the Klan had backed out of their commitment to purchase Stealthshooters, at least until the heat died down over the murders, which they didn't want to be linked to.

For that matter, Crosley doubted he'd be able to find anyone in the state willing to do business with him as long as the murders were getting so much media attention. There was a ragtag band of white supremacists down in New Orleans he figured he could still get to buy a couple crates of the guns, no questions asked, but beyond that it looked as if he were back to playing the waiting game, and after so many years of biding his time, the thought of another delay didn't set too well with him.

"I swear, Evan, you look like you got a boll weevil gnawin' on your gizzard. Wanna talk about it?"

Crosley glanced up from his drink. He was sitting on the front porch of a century-old plantation he now called home. In the wicker rocker across from him was Senator Reese Calhoun, a robust-looking man in his early sixties and one of two Southern Democrats with an eye on the presidential nomination in the party's upcoming summer convention. Calhoun peered at Crosley over the rims of his bifocals, a look of concern on his face.

"Oh, it's nothing really," Crosley told the senator. "Just racking my brains trying to figure out a way to get you in the White House."

Calhoun laughed, deep and heartily. "Well, that explains it all. Me, my ulcer's puttin' in overtime on the same damn business."

"You talked to Hobst again?" Crosley asked, referring to Louisiana's flamboyant governor.

Calhoun nodded as he refreshed his drink with another shot of bourbon. "No way in hell he's gonna bow out in my favor."

"Too bad, because if you both go through the primaries you're just going to cancel each other out and give the whole ball of wax to Abernathy."

"Yep, that's the sad damn truth, Evan."

Thomas Abernathy was a liberal congressman from Ohio and the assumed frontrunner in the Democratic field so long as Hobst and Calhoun continued to split the conservative vote.

"I have to say, Evan," Calhoun went on after he'd primed himself with another round of bourbon, "when you invited me out here today I was kinda expectin' something a little more concrete on your part."

"I've got a check made out to your campaign in the hallway," Crosley reminded the senator.

"I know that." Calhoun smiled thinly and lowered his voice, even though the two men were quite alone on the porch. "But I've heard rumors you've got a few things up your sleeve that might prove to be a tad more influential than a mere donation . . . not that a little hard currency doesn't come in handy, of course."

"Of course." Crosley slowly stood and stretched. His invitation to Calhoun had been extended a week ago before the mass murders. He was going to explain how he knew some hell-raisers in New Orleans who might be interested in pulling a few dirty tricks on Hobst if the price was right. But since those were the same hell-raisers waiting to buy two crateloads of hot Stealthshooters, Crosley thought better of dragging the senator into the transaction. He eyed Calhoun and promised, "Once I tie up a few loose ends I'll give you the full lowdown, but I'm the superstitious type. Don't wanna jinx things by jumping the gun, ya know. I just wanted you to rest assured I'm still in your camp."

"Never doubted that for a second, Evan." Calhoun got up from the rocker and thumped Crosley on the back. "You helped get me back in the Senate two years ago, after all. I'm not likely to forget that overnight."

Crosley grinned. "I remember it myself every time I take a good look around here."

Both men chuckled as they headed down the steps to Calhoun's limo. Crosley had gotten the plantation for a song in return for the strings he'd pulled in helping to get Calhoun reelected to the Senate after a brief "retirement" that he'd taken to avoid a major Washington scandal that would have enveloped him had he remained in a position of high visibility on Capitol Hill.

Calhoun slipped into the back seat of the limo and waved a farewell to Crosley as the vehicle started down the quarter mile of driveway leading to the main road. "Be in touch, Even, hear?"

"You can count on it, Senator."

As he started back up the front walk, Crosley noticed a manservant standing in the doorway.

"Phone call for you, sir," the other man said. "Long distance from New York. An Ahmed Khoury."

Crosley perked up immediately. "I'll take it in the study, Horace," he said as he bounded up the steps, trying to restrain his excitement. If Ahmed Khoury was calling, it could mean only one thing.

The Shiites wanted to buy some guns....

8

It was night.

From his hotel room in downtown Birmingham, Cowboy Kissinger had a clear view of Vulcan holding aloft his glowing torch atop Red Mountain. To his surprise, two blocks away he could also see the nation's largest reproduction of the Statue of Liberty, illuminated on top of the ten-story Liberty National Life Insurance Building. Their oversize grandeur seemed somehow inappropriate in light of the events that had shattered the city in recent days. How could such carnage have bloodied the land under the watchful eyes of such giants?

Kissinger moved away from the window when a phone jangled to life on the nightstand beside his unmade bed. He got to it on the third ring.

"Yeah..."

"John, it's Hal."

"Hi, chief." Kissinger's voice was flat, drained of emotion. "You come up with anything?"

"Negative," Brognola reported. "Kurtzman's been riding the computers since you guys first called in, but he can't come up with anything on Crosley since his death notice five years ago. We've got a man checking with the coroner's office up there to see if there's anything out of order on the death certificate. He's going to take a long look at the info on Crosley's dental charts. If the guy's alive, those charts had to be tampered with.''

"I'd bet on it," Kissinger said.

"It's a five-year-old trail, Cowboy," Brognola reminded the armorer. "I wouldn't get my hopes up."

"Well, I know he's alive and unless he's skipped town I'd bet my life he's still in Birmingham," Kissinger insisted. "One way or another, I'm going to find him and get some answers."

There was a pause on the line before Brognola continued, "Just how well did you know this Crosley guy?"

"Not well enough, obviously." For the past few hours Kissinger hadn't been able to think of much else besides his relationship with Howie Crosley. How could he have let himself be so totally duped? "Is there something you aren't telling me, chief?"

"Afraid so." Brognola waited another beat, then went on. "Seems that up to the time he allegedly died, Crosley was moonlighting for the mob."

"What?"

"Apparently he was some kind of conduit for gambling winnings," Brognola explained. "He passed funds to mules headed for Switzerland on business for a so-called friend. Your basic laundering operation. Story is Crosley died before he could make another delivery and the mob figured their cash went up in the blaze."

"I got a feeling it went south instead," Kissinger said. "Along with my plans for the QA-18."

"It sure seems to add up that way. We'll stay on it, John, but there's a few other things that need going over in the meantime."

"Fire away." Kissinger sat down on the edge of the bed and poured the last of his cola into a drinking glass. He took a sip as Brognola's voice droned on through the receiver.

"First off, we've got the FOG-M here at the farm. I can get it down to you if you're going to be there awhile, otherwise we'll just lock it up and wait till you get back."

"Send it down," Kissinger requested. "Who knows how long this is going to take, and it might be nice to have something else to concentrate on when I need a breather."

"Will do. I'll throw in the Barrett, too, if you want."

"Sure. While you're at it, I could also use some of my tools. I've got a backup set packed for travel at the warehouse. Roger will know where it is."

Brognola murmured under his breath as he jotted the information down. "Gotcha, but this is shaping up to be quite a bit of hardware. I think I'll have Kurtzman get in touch with Coe down there and see if the FBI can't set you up with some temporary work space. Wouldn't go over too well to have the maid come across all this when she comes to make your bed."

"Good point," Kissinger conceded. "What else?"

"We got a call in from Mike Armstrong down in New Orleans an hour ago," Brognola said, referring to a retired FBI agent who periodically lent support to Able Team on assignments on the Gulf Coast. "He's caught wind of rumors that a few strays are putting ARC back into circulation."

The Aryan Right Coalition was one of the countless racist rat packs that had sprung up throughout the South as a more radical alternative to the John Birch Society and the Ku Klux Klan. Founded by redneck bouncer Delbert Gunther, ARC, also known as the White Right, had earned notoriety several months ago with their aborted attempt to selectively poison parts of New York

City's water supply with toxic nuclear wastes stolen from a Louisiana storage facility. Able Team had been responsible for preventing ARC from carrying out their plan, and Gunther had died in the same shoot-out that had supposedly eliminated the organization's paltry membership.

"Well, I've only been down here a few hours and I've seen enough hate around to start up a dozen thug clubs," Kissinger said.

"I don't doubt that, but I think we should take a special interest in this group down in New Orleans."

"Why's that, chief?"

"Armstrong said the rumor he's been hearing is that ARC's planning to arm itself with a cache of weapons from a dealer in Birmingham...."

"Bingo."

"Bingo is right," Brognola said. "My gut feeling is it's more than coincidence. If this Crosley's alive and trying to peddle those QA-18s, odds are he's the one ARC's dealing with. I want you guys operating under that premise at any rate. Look, is Lyons there? I want to lay out a game plan with him."

Kissinger sighed. "Sorry, chief. He's out."

"What about Schwarz or Blancanales?"

"They're out, too."

"Where?" There was an angry, threatening tone in Brognola's voice.

Kissinger got up from the bed and carried the phone back near the window. As he stared out at the streets below, he said, "They had a little unofficial police business to attend to...."

A LOT OF OFF-DUTY COPS in Birmingham did their drinking at the Oxbow, a disheveled hole-in-the-wall five minutes from the downtown station. It was run by a square-jawed, sixty-year-old woman by the name of Peg, who'd earned the distinction of being widowed by not one but three different police officers over the years. As local legend had it, although all three husbands had died under varying circumstances in the line of duty, a common curse had claimed them all. Any cop fool enough to wed Peg again would be signing their death certificate the same time they scrawled their name on the marriage license. Cynical and hardened by the shit-hand life had dealt her, Peg played along with the legend. She warned any cop who fell behind on paying off his drinking tab at the Oxbow that he was apt to wake up some morning to find Peg and a justice of the peace in his bedroom, ready to recite vows and unleash the curse.

Donnie Welch was sitting at a corner table with his partner and a third officer whose barrel chest matched the dimensions of the beer kegs that lined the back wall. All three men were out of uniform, dressed in casual attire. Honky-tonk music was pumping out of a corner jukebox, and the air was thick with cigarette smoke that almost, but not quite, masked the smell left by those poor souls who had lost their lunches after one too many brews. The rest of the bar was crowded with locals, and the buzz of conversation centered around the killing spree south of the city earlier that day.

"You shoulda seen the way Donnie put that fucker away," Welch's partner, Al, boasted. "Bam! Right between the fucking shoulder blades."

"Guess you guys oughta start callin' me 'judge,'" Donnie drawled as he emptied the last bit of beer from a quart pitcher. He put on the same show of mock innocence he'd peddled to the press earlier. "Of course, as we all know, I was merely preventing an escape."

"Yeah, right," the fat cop chortled.

"With God as my witness, Vance," Welch said, raising one hand as if swearing on a Bible. He was sitting so that he faced the front entrance, and his expression quickly soured as he spotted three familiar figures stroll into the Oxbow.

CARL LYONS FELT a twinge of déjà vu as he entered the bar and took in its hard-edged ambience. A lifetime ago he'd spent his share of time in a similar dive with fellow LAPD officers, trying to drink the edge off a rough day on the streets. He was struck by the irony that now he was here to make sure that another set of cops wouldn't be able to sweep today's shift under the rug.

"Over there," he told Gadgets and Blancanales, pointing out the table where Donnie sat with Vance and Al.

As Able Team threaded through the crowd, a Ronnie Milsap tearjerker finished playing on the jukebox and an uneasy silence settled over the bar. The regulars didn't like the looks of the newcomers, and their wary gazes followed the trio to Donnie's corner.

"Well, well, well, if it isn't Kraut, Spic and Span," Welch taunted. "How'd you guys find us?"

"We followed the smell," Lyons said.

Donnie calmly finished his beer, then deadpanned, "Funny man. Uncle Sam know you're up past your bedtime?"

"Back in your squad car this afternoon we made a date," Lyons reminded the cop. "We're here to keep it."

"Oh, I see." Welch glanced over at Al and Vance as he eased back in his chair and cracked his bony knuckles. "I promised these boys we'd give them a chance to visit the hospital and get a transfusion of some good Alabama blood. You guys wanna help me send 'em there?''

Al and Vance sized up Able Team. In terms of sheer bulk they knew there was no contest and that was good enough for Birmingham's finest.

"Glad to," Vance said.

"Count me in," Al seconded.

As the three cops pushed back their chairs and stood, Peg slipped out from behind the bar and quickly placed herself between the opponents. At most she might have weighed just a little more than half of Carl Lyons's 190 pounds, but she showed no sign of being intimidated by any of the men. She took in all six bruisers with one sweeping gaze of her small, fiery eyes, then pointed to the rear door and uttered an insistent one-word command.

"Outside!"

Donnie grinned at the female dynamo, then motioned his colleagues toward the exit. "You heard the gal."

As Able Team followed the cops through the doorway, Peg formed a human barricade to prevent anyone else from leaving, warning the others, "You know the rules. Fair fights only."

"Fair, my ass," one of the locals snickered. "I got ten bucks says those out-of-towners are beef stew inside of five minutes."

"I bet five it'll only take half that time," another regular wagered.

A naked bulb battled the alley's darkness with sixty meager watts of light, leaving plenty of shadows to keep the rats and garbage out of view. Donnie and his counterparts stepped clear of the concrete steps leading down from the bar and spread out as Able Team joined them on the asphalt.

"No hardware," Lyons told the cops, laying down ground rules.

"Yeah," Pol said with a grin as he started rolling up his sleeves. "Strictly come as you are."

"Fine by us," Vance replied on behalf of the home team. He stripped down to a T-shirt to give his opponents a better idea of the musclebound girth they were going to have to deal with. Donnie and Al contented themselves with loosening a few shirt buttons.

"I'll take the beaner," Al said, indicating Blancanales.

"He's mine," Vance decided as he squared off opposite Gadgets. Donnie regarded Lyons with mirthful contempt.

"Well, blondie, I guess that leaves you for me."

None of the men of Able Team had spoken since leaving the Oxbow. Instead, they had devoted their full concentration to surveying the battleground in hope of neutralizing any "home court advantage" the cops might bring into play. Although it was hard for them to see beyond the dull glow of the light over the bar door, it looked as if the alley ran between two side streets. Plenty of room to move now, and a way out in a hurry later if Peg's warning didn't prevent the other locals from charging outside to tip the scales.

The three cops were veteran street brawlers, and they all struck modified boxing stances, crouched slightly forward, hands tightened into fists in front of their faces. Donnie spat tobacco juice as he bobbed lightly in place before Lyons, who stood loosely in the alley, as if uncommitted to the pending conflict.

"Ready when you are, faggot," Welch baited. "Come on, take your best shot."

In hand-to-hand combat Lyons had always preferred shotokan karate in its purest form, but over the years he'd modified techniques to complement his instinctive fighting style. As he stood before Donnie, he counted off to himself in quick sequence and turned his body into an instrument of martial precision. One second he was snapping into a traditional karate stance and drawing in a measured breath, the next he was exhaling a loud cry and subjecting Donnie to a sudden flurry of swiping arms and legs.

Donnie was caught off guard from the first. A sharp jolt of pain surged down his forearm as he absorbed the first blow from Lyons's right foot. The heel of the Ironman's left palm cracked one of the lean cop's ribs a split second later, all but immobilizing him.

Al and Vance were similarly overwhelmed by the unexpected displays of bo jitsu and monkey kung fu demonstrated by Blancanales and Schwarz respectively.

"Hey, lay off with the fucking Bruce Lee shit," Al groaned as he picked himself off the pavement and warily eyed the coiled enemy posed before him.

"Yeah," Vance said, turning away from Gadgets long enough to slip on a set of brass knuckles taken from his pants pocket. As he slowly stood back up, he tried to ignore the throbbing pain where he'd been cuffed on the head by Schwarz's flying feet. "Fight like a man!" he yelled, dropping back into a boxer's pose.

"Suit yourselves," Lyons said, speaking for his associates as he closed his hands into fists and waited for Donnie to come forward.

Limiting themselves to fighting with their fists, Able Team lost the element of surprise that had so decisively marked their initial foray, but their agility was still a potent foil to the plodding street-brawl moves of the off-duty officers. However, when the cops did land punches they were persuasive, especially those backed by the brass knuckles that all three men had managed to slip on during the early exchanges. Lyons caught a roundhouse right that felt as if it broke his jaw, and Blancanales felt blood streaming down his face from where Al's gilded fist had laid open a gash above his right eye.

"Look, as long as you guys want to break the rules, you'll just have to get used to taking a little of what you dish out." Schwarz ducked a left hook and reverted to kung fu, taking out Vance at the knees and following up with a quick series of hard chops from both hands that wreaked hell on the cop's collarbone.

"Right on," Blancanales agreed, taking one last punch to the shoulder before bo-jitsuing Al into quick submission.

Before Donnie could go down like his sidekicks, he reeled away from Lyons and grabbed at his ankles for a .22 pistol secreted in his cowboy boots. He whipped the gun out and was about to fire at Lyons when his hand suddenly jerked to one side, struck sharply by a hurled trash can lid. The gun went off but fired wildly.

"You fucking piece of shit," Lyons said, stepping forward and delivering a karate blow that sent Donnie to dreamland. The Ironman picked up the cop's .22 and threw it across the alley as he told Blancanales, "Nice Frisbee toss, Pol."

"My pleasure," the jitsu master replied. "Little thing I picked up years ago."

Lyons rubbed his jaw and started to walk away. "I think we made our point," he muttered. "Let's get out of here."

Gadgets loomed over the three fallen officers. "So much for the master race, eh, white bread?"

"You're dead," Donnie threatened, nursing a welt below his split lip.

"Funny, I don't feel dead." Gadgets turned to Blancanales. "Hey, homes, you dead?"

"Naw, I'm not dead," Blancanales said. He tapped a bruise on his forehead and shook his head. "Man, I've had bee stings that hurt more than this. Of course, we may feel differently if Hal hears about our little encounter."

The rear door to the Oxbow swung open, spilling more light into the alley. Peg stepped outside and wrinkled her face into an expression of contempt at the sight of the three cops still on the ground. "You pantywaists know what's good for you, you won't show your faces in here for a coupla days. Got that? You're all a disgrace to the uniform."

"Go easy on 'em, lady," Lyons advised. "They're gonna be too busy eating their words to worry about drinking, anyway...."

9

It had been almost twenty years since Hurricane Camille had assaulted the Gulf shores of Louisiana with its two-hundred-mile-an-hour winds and two-story tidal waves. It had wiped out more than five thousand residences in its concentrated fury and turned much of the Plaque-mines Parish alluvial fan into a desolate wasteland of splintered homes, twisted automobiles and broken dreams. Some of the survivors had come back to resettle small hamlets such as Buras, Triumph and Boothville, but others had been so dispirited by their losses that they had left behind the ruins of their former lives and sought better tomorrows elsewhere. Vast expanses of the rangy peninsula had remained undeveloped over the years, with the refuse of Camille strewn across marshlands and gently rolling plains. Nature moved in to reclaim aban-doned homesteads, layering concrete-slabbed founda-tions with moss and weeds. Penniless squatters roamed the more accessible wastes and settled into any half-standing structure whose walls, however flimsy, might still help blunt the chill of night and the fall of rain.

Other stretches of land, surrounded by meandering, alligator-infested swamps, proved too uninviting for va-grants. It was here, in this unstable no-man's-land, that Delbert Gunther, founder of the Aryan Right Coalition, had undergone his most memorable period of paramili-

tary training under the supervision of Sergeant Stan
Drago. Drago's Mercenary Operations School had been
by far one of the most genuine and thorough of the many
trendy, privately run outfits throughout the nation that
offered instruction in basic survival skills, hand-to-hand
combat techniques and military strategies that could be
applied to situations ranging from fending off frantic
neighbors during food shortages to guerrilla insurgency.

Drago had served as Gunther's mentor, showing him
how to kill, how to subsist on whatever diet the environment provided and how to take charge of any given situation and maintain a position of command.

Gunther had been a good pupil, using his gained expertise to weld together his small but tightly woven and
determined band of White Rightists. Drago contented
himself on the sidelines as far as the ARC was concerned, but when Gunther and his most trusted cohorts
had died during their failed attempt to sabotage Facility
Six of New York City's Municipal Water District, there
was a sudden leadership gap that had proved too tempt-
ing to resist. The sergeant had moved in, seized control
and quickly taken the remaining membership underground to avoid the inevitable dragnet by law-
enforcement agencies hoping to mop up in the aftermath of Gunther's demise.

ARC had retreated to Plaquemines Parish to lick its
wounds, taking over the remote site that had formerly
served as headquarters for Drago's Mercenary Operations School. The latter outfit had been incorporated into
ARC as its guerrilla warfare arm, becoming an outlaw
equivalent of the military's special forces.

Drago was surprised at how quickly he'd been able to
whip the unit into shape. Of the fifteen men who had
started out the rigorous weeks of training, ten were still

going strong. Now he watched them with admiration as they took their allotted breather for the morning, caked with mud from crawling on their bellies since dawn in a mock infiltration exercise. Their intended target, less than a hundred yards away, was an oysterman's shack, rising on wooden stilts from the surrounding marsh-lands. A dock reached out into the clear blue water that coursed erratically around scattered spits of land. Moored to the dock was a weatherbeaten hydrofoil, one of the few vehicles capable of traversing this part of the country on a year-round basis.

The wind shifted slightly, bringing with it an acrid smell from the mines at Port Sulphur, miles to the south.

"Hey, who cut the fucking cheese?" Rob Aames, the oldest recruit, complained, half grinning.

Another of the men, whose fatigues were the least soiled of the group, sniffed the air around him and waved one hand to take the blame, "Gee, guys, I'm sorry. Musta been those snakes we had for breakfast."

"I told you to cook yours a little longer, Gus," Aames razzed his cohort as he extracted a pair of palm-sized binoculars from a clipcase on his belt and peered over the grass at the distant shack. "Hey, hey, Sarge, looks like we're in luck. I count three jigs on the dock."

"Shit," Drago muttered, wading through the shallow water to Rob's side and taking the binoculars. "They're supposed to be hauling oysters into Bohemia today. What the fuck are they still doing out here?"

"No prob, Sarge," Rob said. "We can just do 'em in when we storm the place."

"No way," Drago replied coldly, focusing on the blacks near the shack.

"Why not?" another one of the recruits wanted to know. "Who the hell's gonna miss a few stray niggers out here in the middle of goddamn nowhere?"

Drago lowered the glasses and eyed his men. "This is just an exercise, remember? We'll wait here until they leave, then finish up."

"Whoop-dee-doo," Aames muttered, sitting back down on the embankment and rotating his index finger in the air. "Six hours we been slinkin' around like gators, just so's we can go up to that friggin' shack and touch the stilts like we're playing a goddamn game of kick-the-can."

Drago took a quick stride to his left, coming up on Rob before the man had a chance to react. The sergeant whipped out a hunting knife with a six-inch blade and pressed the tip lightly against Aames's jugular. "You got a problem with that, soldier?"

Rob's eyes rolled downward, taking in the glint of sunlight off the blade's edge. All around Drago the other recruits tensed.

"It's just that I thought our whole purpose was supposed to put the niggers back in their place," Aames explained, showing no fear of the knife. "No offense, Sarge, but we ain't done nothing these past two months but slop through the mud around here like pigs at playtime."

"You got a problem with that, soldier?" Drago repeated.

Rob hesitated before replying. When he swallowed, he could feel the raw steel creeping deeper into his neck. "No," he finally whispered hoarsely.

"No what?"

"No, sir."

Drago pulled the knife away from Aames's throat and resheathed it, glaring at the other men for any trace of mutiny in their eyes. "Anyone else think we're not going through with these drills for a reason?"

The others were silent, unmoving. The youngest in the group, twenty-year-old Louis Billingsworth, struggled to retain his composure. He wanted nothing better than to throw down his weapon and declare he'd had enough. But he kept quiet instead, knowing the probable consequences of backing out now.

"The warrior that wins is the one that chooses his battles carefully," Drago told the recruits. "I figure another couple days and we'll be ready to make our move, and when we do, we aren't going to screw around knocking off niggers in the boondocks. Any fucking yahoo can do that. No, we're after a much bigger fish. Much bigger..."

Drago's brief sermon was interrupted by the revving of the hydrofoil's motor. He watched as the boatload of blacks headed off in the opposite direction, then signaled for his men to get on their feet.

"Okay," he said, "let's wrap this up and get back to the base. I heard a rumor Bobby Lee was going out for beer and steaks while we were gone...."

"All right!" the lean recruit said as he fit a bayonet to the end of his rifle. The others did the same, readying for the simulated siege of the distant shack. The rifles were old Belgian FNs, longtime staples among NATO forces fond of the weapon's simplicity and durability. Set on automatic, the FN could spit out 7.62 mm bullets from a 20-round magazine at the rate of 600 rpm. Self-loading and fully waterproof, the rifles were particularly useful in the marshland environment where ARC based its operations.

However, for the big mission that Drago was putting together, Belgian FNs were too loud and too conspicuous to be of any use. What he needed was a cache of smaller weapons for the men. In particular, he needed a supply of good semiautomatic pistols with built-in silencers and flash suppressors. Provided this Crosley guy in Birmingham didn't let him down, he'd soon have his hands on just such weapons.

10

FBI agent Ross Coe had requisitioned a back room at the Birmingham field office for Kissinger's use while he was in town. Both Kissinger and Blancanales were on hand when the shipment from Stony Man Farm arrived under heavy security. Lyons and Schwarz were already on their way to New Orleans for a rendezvous with Mike Armstrong.

"I hope you guys aren't aiming to start a war on us down here," Coe remarked as he watched Cowboy unpack the FOG-M missile and Barrett M-82. "Seems you've already ruffled a few feathers with our boys in blue."

"We just had a score to settle with a few bad apples," Blancanales assured the agent. "We've got no problems with the rest of the barrel."

"Glad to hear it."

"What is this baby, anyway?" Coe was eyeing the FOG-M. "Looks like Vulcan's pecker."

"If it is, you better stand clear when he gets his rocks off," Pol cracked as he gave Kissinger a hand transferring the missile to a workbench. The room was roughly half the size of Kissinger's shop back at the farm. There were no windows, and the cinder-block walls gave the enclosure an institutional feel. Recessed lights in the acoustically tiled ceiling gave off a steady fluorescent glow.

"Like I told your boss, we'll lend what help we can trying to track down Crosley, but it's going to be a bit of the needle-in-a-haystack routine, I'm afraid." Coe tapped the barrel of the Barrett M-82, still resting in its packing crate. "Birmingham's got more manufacturing plants than just about anyplace on the map, and most of 'em have the facilities for piecing together weapon parts. And as for Crosley himself, his prints haven't shown up on file, so whatever kind of cover he's established for himself, he's been keeping his nose clean."

"We'll take whatever help we can get," Kissinger said. He opened a small leather carrying case and took out the murder weapon Harlan Carruthers had dropped at the zoo. "Hopefully once I strip this down and go over it with a fine-tooth comb we'll be able to narrow the field."

"Well, you know where my office is if you come up with something." Coe headed for the door along with the three field agents who had helped move Kissinger's things into the spare room. "I've got two of my best men backing me up. One of 'em's doing background checks on Carruthers, and the other's sniffing around gunsmith shops. We'll let you know if we come up with anything."

"And vice versa," Pol promised.

Left alone, it took both Kissinger and Blancanales to hoist the oversize trunk filled with Cowboy's spare gunsmithing tools. They set it on the workbench, and Pol discreetly looked the other way while Kissinger worked the combination on the latch locks. He picked up the QA-18 and looked at it closely for the first time.

"It may be your design, Cowboy, but it's sure easy to see you didn't make this one."

"Why's that?"

"Workmanship just doesn't match up to yours," Blancanales said. "Lotta burred screws and rough edges."

Kissinger smiled wryly. "I didn't think you guys really noticed that stuff."

"Guess again, *amigo*." Blancanales handed the gun to Kissinger. "If we didn't go out there with the best hardware going, you can bet your sweet ass Able Team would be six feet under doin' a worm dance. Why do you think we waited so long gettin' by on Konzaki's leftovers before we brought you in? We wanted the best, not just any damn tinkerer."

"I'm flattered," Kissinger admitted. He looked over the QA-18 and sighed wistfully. "Yeah, you should have seen my prototype of this. I cleaned and polished that thing so much it damn near glowed in the dark."

"Before this is over, I got a feeling we'll all get a chance to see what it looked like," Blancanales said.

"You're right there."

Kissinger eyeballed the main screw slots of the weapon and sorted through his tools for a screwdriver to match the groove. As his colleague had correctly observed, it was attention to the small details that differentiated Kissinger's craftsmanship from whoever had resurrected his QA-18 from the drawing board. Cowboy's guess was that Crosley had linked up with some illicit manufacturer to make the handgun—someone who was more interested in profit margins than precision. Probably someone who also put out a lot of Saturday Night Specials, those ineptly made weapons that served little purpose other than to provide two-bit hoodlums with a chance to earn a murder rap during the commission of other crimes.

"I know you don't like people looking over your shoulder when you work," Blancanales told the gunsmith. "I think I'll track down a yellow pages and let my fingers do a little walking through the gun shops. Shouldn't take more than a few questions to figure out which places are sloppy about their smith work, right?"

"Just make sure you aren't duplicating Coe's work," Cowboy said. "We don't want to tip our hand before we get a chance to play it."

"Sí," Pol replied on his way out the door. "Catch you later."

Kissinger tossed off a quick wave, then turned his full attention to the QA-18 on the workbench. Working at the screws, he felt a little like Pandora getting ready to pry into the forbidden box. Here was a symbol of a past he'd tried his best to forget, thinking that he'd never be able to recover the lost work that had gone into his pride and joy. Now, however shabbily constructed it was, his "baby" was back in his hands. Once he had a look at the inner workings of the gun, all the details he'd forgotten came rushing back to him and, absorbed in his work, he almost felt as if he were back in Wisconsin and on the verge of big things. . . .

11

Ahmed Khoury was a New York lawyer with American citizenship, but his primary allegiance was to Lebanon and the most feared offshoot of that country's militant Shiite cell, the Hizbullah. His legal expertise had served the Hizbullah cause well over the years, pinpointing the various loopholes and guaranteed freedoms in American law books that allowed his people to spread their propaganda and build a network of terrorist cells throughout the States with a certain ease and impunity. It was through Khoury's assistance that a Hizbullah assassin named Kadal had nearly succeeded in pulling off a planned execution of the President of the United States, the prime minister of Israel and anti-Shiite members of a Muslim delegation to a Trilateral Compact meeting that had been held in New York several months ago. Ironically it had been Able Team that had thwarted Kadal, dispatching him to Allah in a blaze of gunfire that had rocked the dock area of New York's West Side.

Khoury had adequately covered his tracks and avoided any association with Kadal in the aftermath of that incident, but when it came to furthering the Hizbullah cause, the lawyer didn't subscribe to the notion that once bitten, twice shy. If anything, Kadal's failure had only prompted Khoury and his minions in the Middle East to seek out an even fiercer retribution against the enemies of Islam.

The national headlines in America provided him with his answer. Down south in Forsyth County, Georgia, an all-white community had been aided by the Ku Klux Klan in disrupting a civil rights march protesting local segregation. Out in California a nineteen-year-old had been arrested for burning a cross on the front lawn of a black family. In New York the Howard Beach death of a black youth chased into traffic by a gang of hostile whites was still a source of controversy. And a group calling itself the Aryan Right Coalition had attempted to poison a water reservoir servicing the more ethnically mixed neighborhoods in Manhattan. These incidents were only the tip of a much larger iceberg called racial hatred.

Khoury knew all about such hatred because he was a swarthy-skinned native of Lebanon. He was often the victim of vindictive epithets cast his way by reactionary white Americans looking to vent their anger on some likely scapegoat for their personal problems. He'd been mistaken for a Syrian, an Iranian, a Libyan, and he'd been called everything from camel jockey and olive-eater to names he tried his best not to remember.

But as he pieced together his new plan, Ahmed Khoury took satisfaction in the knowledge that the last laugh would be his. The Hizbullah had decided that rather than risk exposing themselves before they had had a chance to fully entrench themselves in America, they could accomplish many of their goals merely by getting Americans to turn their hate toward one another and escalate that hate into violence. The Shiites would like nothing better than to see the United States torn from within by the sort of racial unrest that had led to the riots of Watts, Detroit and Newark in the sixties. Properly exploited, the resulting chaos and anarchy would drain the resources of local authorities and thereby give the Muslim terrorists greater flexibility in implementing their own brand of guerrilla warfare.

Khoury had already set up several dummy corporations to channel Muslim funds into racist organizations such as the John Birch Society, Ku Klux Klan and Minutemen. Of course, these groups had no idea they were getting donations from the very sort of people their hate was directed against. The dummy corporations were invariably structured to give the appearance of being philanthropic outfits backed by predominantly white concerns, and as a rule the Klan and its kindred associates didn't look their gift horses in the mouth. Usually form letters would be sent out with words of thanks for the initial contribution and then periodic news flyers would be circulated with requests for additional acts of charity.

Overall, though, Khoury was impatient with the apparent timidity of the more prominent right-wing organizations, who seemed more concerned with ideological ranting and fund-raising than with taking action. And so he'd sent his underlings across the country to sniff out splinter groups who seemed more likely to put their might where their mouths were when it came time to follow through. True, the Klan might put on their hoods and club a few demonstrators here and there, but Khoury and the Shiites wanted more than that.

They wanted blood.

They wanted war in the streets of America, with Americans killing one another over the issue of race.

The search for an unwitting ally hadn't taken long.

Khoury's envoy in New Orleans, Hakim Shrevi, a light-skinned Muslim whose ability to pass for white had made him an invaluable middleman over the years, had learned that the Aryan Right Coalition had reassembled. The new man in charge was an ex-marine named Stan Drago who seemed ready to have ARC wreak whatever hell it could on its avowed enemies once it had resources to do so.

It had been Hakim Shrevi, calling himself Peter Stevens, who had recently approached Sergeant Drago on behalf of an anonymous benefactor who wished to make a substantial contribution to ARC, provided it would use a portion of that money to undertake a particularly sensitive mission.

That mission was to assassinate Governor Lowell Hobst of Louisiana, and to make it look as if the murder had been done by a group of black extremists. Drago had had no problem understanding the rationale and strategy behind such a move. It would be a way of killing two birds with one stone. With Hobst eliminated from contention for the upcoming presidential nomination, the conservative vote would gravitate toward Alabama's Reese Calhoun. Furthermore, by pinning Hobst's death on black extremists, Calhoun's somewhat racist reputation wouldn't be quite so apt to lose him votes in more moderate states around the nation. If anything, the expected backlash against blacks would likely improve his chances of making it to the White House.

Drago was shrewd enough to suspect a possible trap, and he had refused to respond to Shrevi's proposal until he'd had a chance to check out the man's background and credentials. Fortunately for Shrevi, his identity as Peter Stevens was linked to all the dummy corporations through which Ahmed Khoury had placed his earlier contributions with the Ku Klux Klan and John Birch Society. With references like that, Shrevi's cover had stood up cleanly, and a deal had been made.

Although he had not divulged any particulars regarding the mechanics of the assassination, Drago had requested good-faith money up front as well as follow-up funds for the purchase of special weapons he thought he'd need for the operation. When Shrevi had subsequently heard Drago discuss the special features of the Grossler Stealthshooters he wanted to buy from an illicit dealer in Birmingham, the Muslim had been hard-pressed to remain composed. Here was a weapon that seemed ideal for the needs of his people as well, both here in America and back in the Middle East.

It had been Shrevi's excited report back to Ahmed Khoury in New York that had led to negotiations between Khoury and Evan Grossler for the purchase of five hundred Stealthshooters. Grossler had no idea that there was a connection between his two most recent clients, and Khoury expected to keep it that way.

Now, two weeks later, Hakim Shrevi was back in New Orleans, riding in the back of a sleek white limousine as it turned off Highway 610 onto Marconi Drive, which led into the vast expanse of City Park. Giant oaks trailed great clumps of Spanish moss from their gnarled limbs. Out on the wide stream that wound its way throughout the park, Shrevi could see people in rowboats and pontoons, enjoying the breezeless, sunny afternoon. *How peaceful and innocent they all seem,* Shrevi thought to himself as he reached for the cellular phone that had just blinked on. *If the poor deluded fools only knew...*

He answered the phone in his native tongue, knowing that Ahmed Khoury preferred to avoid using English whenever possible. The lawyer wanted a progress report. Shrevi calmly explained that the rendezvous hadn't taken place yet. He promised to call Khoury in New York as soon as there was news.

The limo pulled into the main parking lot. Vehicles of all sizes and descriptions were parked in neat rows on either side of a landscaped traffic island. Both Shrevi and his driver looked for the late-model Olds that was supposed to meet them here. There were a couple cars matching that rough description, but neither were occupied.

"Late," Shrevi murmured to himself, glancing at the gold Rolex on his wrist.

"There," the driver said, gesturing through the windshield at an Olds that had just pulled into the lot. The other vehicle circled around the lot before pulling to a stop alongside the limousine. Less than two feet separated the cars. The passenger's window in the front seat of the Olds was rolled down, and Stan Drago snapped a cigarette butt out onto the pavement. The flick of a power switch lowered Shrevi's window, and the two men faced each other.

"Long time, no see," Drago drawled, eyeing the limo's polished sheen. "Nice wheels, Stevens."

"You're late."

Drago checked his watch and shrugged. "Two minutes. Big shit. You renting that canoe by the second or something?"

"I hope you take the finer details into consideration when you're fulfilling your mission."

"That's my concern," Drago snapped. "Look, if you're so pressed for time, let's have the money and you can be on your way."

"My superiors would like to know what your plan is," Shrevi said, refusing to lose his composure.

"They'll be able to read about it in the papers when it's over," Drago replied. He lit another cigarette and held one hand halfway out the window. "Now give me the fucking cash before the park cops stroll by on queer patrol, okay?"

Shrevi reached into his suit pocket and removed a sealed envelope. "You'll only get the rest if you succeed," he reminded the mercenary as he passed the cash to Drago.

"Hey, it's not like this is the first job I've handled, Stevens. Cut me some slack, would you?" Drago quickly opened the envelope and counted off the currency. Hundred-dollar bills, an inch thick. As he started to roll up his window, Drago added, "It'll be done by this time tomorrow. I'll hold up my end. You just make sure you've got more of this green stuff ready for me."

Shrevi's window slid upward, and he disappeared from view behind its tinted glass. The Olds stayed put a few seconds while the limo pulled away.

"So far so good," Drago murmured as he recounted the money and slipped it into his pocket. "Okay, let's get the show on the road, Louis."

"Yes, sir," Billingsworth said from the driver's seat. His hands were clutched tightly around the steering wheel, and he hoped Drago wouldn't notice his sweating palms. The young man was paranoid, fearful there was no way he'd get through the week without Drago wising up to his misgivings. And if there was one thing Louis had in his high-strung life now, it was misgivings.

Louis had come into ARC filled with anger at the world in general and blacks specifically. His dad had lost a job due to affirmative action hiring practices a couple of years ago, and Louis's more recent attempts to land a scholarship for college had been unsuccessful, largely because so many funds were earmarked for ethnic groups. He wanted to get back at all those who'd put the chip on his shoulder, and ARC seemed like the best place to do it.

But now he wasn't so sure. After months of being surrounded by older men whose hatred ran even deeper than his own, he'd come to feel a revulsion for all the violence that ARC advocated. Drago still hadn't explained the nature of their upcoming mission to him or to any of the other men, but Louis could easily guess from all the secrecy and the amount of customized semiautomatics being brought in for the job that something heavy was about to go down, something he might well regret being a party to. He kept his reservations to himself, though, having witnessed the brutal beating that had been administered to another recruit who had decided he wanted to bail out of ARC. The guy had lapsed into a coma and died in the barracks a day later. Instead of a burial, he was dragged out into the marshes to a spot where the gators were at their thickest. There was nothing left of him when the group had come back a few hours later after another training exercise. Louis didn't want to fall victim to a similar fate. Not if it could be helped.

"You're gonna love these guns, Louis," Drago said through the smoke he blew as they left the park and headed for Robert E. Lee Boulevard. "Put people away without 'em ever knowing what the hell hit 'em."

"Sounds good," Louis said, trying to sound pleased. "So they're coming in tonight, then?"

"That's right, my man." Drago checked his watch again. "Little less than seven hours."

Louis took note of the time. He already knew the place. Now if he could only get a chance to slip away.

12

Five miles north of Birmingham, Howie Crosley drove his Dodge pickup off the main thoroughfare and maneuvered around the more treacherous chuckholes and washouts on a pair of twin ruts passing for a back road. The pines and dogwoods thickened on either side of him as he sat forward as far as he could to keep an eye on the way before him.

"I sure as hell ain't gonna use this for the Shiites," he told himself, grimacing at the thought of trying to haul five hundred packed Stealthshooters over this terrain without damaging the merchandise. It was bad enough with the two cases on the seat beside him, bundled and cushioned so thickly that he barely had room to drive.

After a half mile the trees thinned out and Crosley reached a meadow. The road vanished in the weeds, but he realized quickly that the ground itself was more level than the ruts he'd been traveling.

The helicopter was already there and waiting, turning the meadow weeds into waves with the whirring play of its rotors. The pilot waved a greeting to Crosley and jumped from the chopper ducking low to avoid the deadly blades as he moved out to the pickup.

"Any problem finding it?" the pilot yelled in order to be heard above the drone of the aircraft. There was Cajun blood in his features, bemusement in his white-toothed smile.

"I'm gonna need new shocks by the time I get back to the main drag," Crosley complained.

"Well, you gotta pay a price for some privacy these days, eh, Mr. Grossler?"

"Maybe you do at that, Cholly."

Before leaving the truck, Crosley leaned his full weight into the parcel beside him, easing it across the seat. Cholly opened the passenger's door and started pulling from the other side. Once he had the bundle halfway out, he waited for Crosley to circle around and give him a hand carrying it the short haul to the copter.

"You remember your orders?" Crosley asked, shouting at the man only a few feet away from him. Cholly still could barely hear him over the engine.

"Sure thing, Mr. Grossler. You can count on Cholly."

"Good." Once the crates were loaded and secured for the flight south, Crosley pulled a money clip from his pocket and removed the folded fifties. "Here. You can count on the rest when you bring me their payment."

Cholly gestured thumbs-up and waited for Crosley to move clear of the helicopter before lifting off. He was flying a small Sikorsky, old but reliable and fast enough to get the contraband down to Mobile before sundown. From there, the arms would be transferred to a small, speedy cabin cruiser belonging to a contact of Drago's. Cholly would be paid off and would fly back while the weapons were shipped to New Orleans and their final destination, the arsenal of the Aryan Right Coalition.

"One down, one to go," Crosley reflected as he got back in the Dodge and began the drive back to Birmingham.

The bigger deal with Khoury and the Shiites would require more planning, more precautions. It could make or break him, depending on how he handled it. One thing was sure, he was going into the deal with his eyes open. A handshake and a man's word didn't hold much water when it came to dealing with a band of fanatics. He had a right to feel slightly paranoid, and as he got back on the highway he considered his options for keeping an upper, or at least even hand.

Enforcers.

That's what he needed. A little extra muscle to back up his own meager security force. He could get back in touch with the Klan...but then again they might veto the whole works once they found out he was dealing with the Shiites. If he wanted to go that route, he'd be better off getting just a few Klansmen to take on a little "unofficial" business without dragging the whole membership into it. Yeah, something like that might work, he thought.

Crosley was coming into Birmingham. He swerved over to the right lane and got off at the next exit, then took a few side streets until he was parked in front of the Oxbow. The car he was looking for, an '84 Firebird in bad need of a wash, was parked in the side lot.

Inside, Crosley found Donnie Welch sitting alone at the far end of the bar, his bruised, swollen face a testimony to the long-term pain a few well-placed karate blows can render.

"Jesus, what happened to you, Donnie?" Crosley asked as he pulled up a stool.

"I went to shave and grabbed the blender by mistake," Welch grumbled, flagging down Peg and pointing to the empty glass in front of him.

"Draw me one, too, willya, Peg?" Crosley asked the owner.

The bar was half empty, with most of the patrons hanging out near a corner television set broadcasting Super Bowl previews. Donnie made sure no one else was listening, then casually told Crosley, "You owe me, Grossler."

"What?"

Peg brought the men their beers and sneered at Donnie even when he motioned for her to keep the change from a fivespot he gave her to bring his tab up to date. The off-duty cop waited until the woman was off washing mugs, then he told Howie, "I took that little shit out of the picture back at the zoo because it looked like he was getting ready to sing."

Crosley was stunned. "But the papers said that—"

"The goddamn papers said what we wanted them to hear." Welch took a long draw off his beer and wiped the foam from his lips. "How the fuck do you think it would have gone over around here if he started talking about how he yanked those guns from you and me and Lucas a couple blocks from here?"

It took Crosley a few moments to put things into perspective. No way was he going to ask Welch for any favors. Not now. "I see," he finally managed to whisper. "Thanks. I'm sure Lucas is grateful, too."

"I'll deal with him on my own later," Donnie said. "I'm not finished with you yet."

"Look," the dealer bartered. "Maybe I can see to it that the Klan gets a free case of Stealthshooters."

"Yeah, maybe you can at that, Crosley."

Howie nearly lost his grip on his beer. This was the first time anyone in Birmingham had ever addressed him by his real name. He turned to Donnie, incredulous, trying feebly to bluff his way out. "What'd you call me?"

"Howard Crosley, to be specific." Welch finished his beer, relishing the other man's uneasiness. Then he pointed to his disfigured face and said, "I got this from some guys who're looking for you."

Crosley's skin paled. He didn't even have to ask for descriptions of the men to know what one of them looked like.

John Kissinger was in town. Crosley could feel it in his bones. It wasn't a pleasant feeling.

13

New Orleans was in the midst of Mardi Gras season, and the streets of the French Quarter thrived on nighttime revelry. It was the first week of parades, and free-spirited souls spilled out from local bars and restaurants to lend their aid to the merriment. Firecrackers popped loudly, giving off a sulfurous smell to rival that given off by sparklers and bargain-basement fireworks let loose from second-story balconies framed in wrought iron. Harmonicas, banjos, snare drums and more varieties of horns than any one man could name, all provided musical accompaniment to the stomping of feet down the cobbled roads and the boisterous singing of participants. Even prior to the start of the parades, as far back as Christmas, the partying had begun, and it would continue unabated until Ash Wednesday the following month, when the Lenten season would begin and people would supposedly deny themselves the pleasures of such rambunctious frivolity.

Carl Lyons had already given up any pretense of cheerfulness. As he and Gadgets Schwarz threaded their way through the joyful sea of humanity, the Ironman was again beset by a sense of gloom and residual grief, for it was here in New Orleans that one of the women in his life had met her doom.

Margie Williams. A pert little psychologist with liberal tendencies, she had seemed the unlikeliest sort of woman for Lyons to get involved with. Their brief relationship had had its share of arguments, but overall it had been a case of opposites attracting. After the ritual of casual dating, they'd gotten serious enough about each other to link up for a romantic tour of California's wine counties. Bad move. There were some tender moments, but spending all their time together had only given them keener awareness of their ultimate incompatibility. After a particularly unpleasant incident at one of the wineries, in which Lyons had treated a pair of unruly bikers to the same going-over that he later inflicted on Birmingham cop Donnie Welch, the couple's ideological differences had come to a head. Margie had packed up and flown to New Orleans for a psychologists' convention. By fateful coincidence, the two bikers Lyons had throttled showed up in Louisiana at the same time, ripe for vengeance against an easy target. Margie had been abducted shortly after leaving the airport. By the time Lyons had tracked her down, she was nothing more than a corpse tucked a few hundred miles away in a decrepit Mexicali morgue.

Lyons eventually caught up with the bikers, whose trip to New Orleans had put them in collusion with Delbert Gunther and ARC. He'd personally seen to their execution during the shoot-out at the water facility in New York, but their deaths had done little to take the edge off his feelings about Margie. Walking down the streets of New Orleans, the Ironman was again plagued by self-recrimination, feeling that if he and Margie hadn't had that one final argument, she wouldn't have come here to die.

True, he had gone on to find another woman to share some time with, and before her own tragic death Julie Harris had, in her own way, become the love of his life. But that didn't take away the pain and sense of loss that had come with Margie's death, any more than Margie's presence had voided his memories of Flor Trujillo, yet another good woman who'd died in the line of his duty.

"Aha!" Gadgets exclaimed, pointing out the entrance to the restaurant where they were due to meet with Mike Armstrong. "Here we are, and not a moment too soon. I think you need a good stiff drink."

"I'll be okay," Lyons insisted.

Brennan's Restaurant had an international reputation, and as Gadgets and Lyons were led through the dining area to their table, they could see and smell the reason. Grillades steamed atop a bed of grits; bananas Foster aglow with the flame of ignited rum; roasted quail in a potato nest; eggs Portuguese and eggs Hussarde with grilled tomatoes; pompano Toulouse and snail omelets—each gourmet dish prepared with the utmost care and set before diners with polished flair. If you liked eating and didn't believe in an afterlife, people said Brennan's was as close as you'd ever get to heaven.

Mike Armstrong was waiting for them in a corner booth, sipping what looked to be a mint julep. A tanned, rugged-looking man in his early sixties, Armstrong wore a straw Stetson with the confidence of a man in charge of his life. Since retiring from the Bureau six years ago, he'd remained a vital figure in the realm of law enforcement, getting a private investigator's license and periodically free-lancing for government agents eager to pick his brains on matters concerning the New Orleans turf he'd prowled for the better part of forty years. He'd gotten calls from Stony Man Farm several times. It had been

Armstrong's sad duty to call Hal Brognola with details about the disappearance of Margaret Williams the day her cab had been run off the road a few miles north of the airport in New Orleans. As he saw Lyons slip into the seat across from him, the ex-agent could see that bad memories weighed the Ironman down. By the same token, he could also sense that Lyons didn't feel like talking about the past.

"Evenin', gents," Armstrong greeted the men simply.

"'lo, Mike," Gadgets said, shaking the older man's hand. Lyons followed suit, exchanging nods with Armstrong, who promptly flagged down a waiter.

Once his guests had ordered drinks and been given menus, Armstrong said, "Well, as we all expected the vermin are back out of the woodwork."

He went on to explain how a raid two months ago on the Aryan Right Coalition's headquarters out near the Bayou des Allemands had come up empty-handed as far as nabbing any members of the organization, although there was enough evidence recovered at the site to confirm the likelihood that there were more White Rightists than those who had been gunned down by Able Team outside New York City. Weeks had passed without any new leads to the whereabouts or activities of the survivors, and it had been assumed that the strays had latched onto other similar organizations or had left the state altogether.

"Then a couple things happened that made us sit up and take notice," Armstrong went on after the drinks had arrived. "I still have a few contacts with the Bureau, and I found out that they'd pegged a link between ARC and the robbery of three crates of old Belgian FNs from a supply depot out near Washington Park a month ago. The security officer on duty took a few rounds in the chest, but he lived long enough to give us a description of the guy running the heist. We figure it's a guy named Stan Drago. Ex-marine who used to run one of these mercenary schools somewhere out in the boonies.''

''How's he tie into ARC?'' Lyons asked between sips of his bourbon. The drink was already helping to loosen him up.

''The Bureau had an informant who spent a couple weeks at Drago's school before it went underground. Guy called Joe. He said Delbert Gunther was in the same class playing teacher's pet.'' Armstrong finished his julep and wiped his lips with a napkin before going on. ''The sheet on Drago makes him look like definite ARC material. He was discharged from the marines for nearly killing a couple of blacks during a routine training exercise, and our pigeon says Drago threw in a lot of racist crap during lectures at his school.''

The waiter showed up to take the men's dinner orders. Lyons and Schwarz both opted for lobster and jumbo shrimp while Armstrong chose Cajun peppersteak. As the waiter took the menus and headed off, Schwarz asked Armstrong, ''What about the Birmingham connection?''

Armstrong's face darkened. ''The Bureau sent this Joe guy out to try and infiltrate ARC. He wasn't able to link up with Drago himself, but he did manage to get referred to somebody else with the outfit. We wired Joe when he went for an interview out by the levee, near Jackson Square.

''He was playing it well, pumping a lot of info about plans, membership, stuff like that. The other guy said that when ARC got back into the thick of things, they were going to do it in a big way. That's when we heard about some semiautomatics being brought in from Birmingham. Joe pressed for more details, and, well..."

"Blew his cover?" Lyons guessed.

Armstrong nodded. "Last thing we heard was somebody joining them on the levee, saying something about Joe asking too many questions. Near as we can figure it, they gave him a quick frisk, then dewired him before they cut his throat. We had backups a couple blocks away, but Joe was in the levee before they could show up. No trace of the others."

"Shit," Lyons swore, shaking his head. "So we don't have a hell of a lot to go with, do we?"

"Well, unless they scrapped their original plans, the deal should be going down tomorrow night. There was mention about boats, so we're going to keep our eyes on the waterways. That still leaves a whole lot of ground to cover, though."

"But that also gives us a day to sniff around," Gadgets countered optimistically. As the waiter returned with a plateful of escargot for their appetizers, he smacked his lips and unfolded a napkin across his lap. He lifted his glass and proposed a toast. "Let's eat, drink and be merry tonight, because tomorrow we're gonna be too goddamn busy to have any fun."

14

Less than two blocks away from where Schwarz and Lyons were dining with Mike Armstrong, Rob Aames, senior member of Drago's ARC guerrilla squad, crushed out a cigarillo under the heel of his lizard-skin boots. He walked down St. Peter Street and discreetly joined the crush of people crowding into Preservation Hall, a converted art gallery-turned-landmark where traditional, unadulterated New Orleans jazz was played nightly. Black-and-white photographs of musical legends lined the pegboard walls, and the only air-conditioning was provided by a pair of ancient upright fans tilted toward the ceiling. As the band warmed up, those patrons unable to find a vacant bench or chair contented themselves with a seat on the wooden floor.

Standing along the back wall, Aames only half listened to the makeshift band of local veterans that soon took over one corner of the main room and began to play some steamy, horn-heavy jazz backed by an upright bass and piano. His attention was primarily on the racially mixed crowd, which took in the music with eager enthusiasm, clapping along on cue from the trombone player—a black man who looked as if he were pushing ninety but played like someone a third his age. As he honked out the last few notes of "When the Saints Go Marching In," someone leaned forward and tossed a five-dollar bill into a porkpie hat set on the floor in front of the band.

"'Poor Man's Blues,'" the patron requested above the applause.

The trombone player eyed the fivespot and grinned. "You pay five dollah for one song, no wonder you poah."

Laughter rippled through the throng, then quickly subsided as the mournful notes from a baritone sax cut through the room. The rest of the band kicked in, building the tune's mournful lament.

Goddamn jig music anyway, Aames thought to himself. If it weren't for so many nigger-lovin' honkies hangin' out with the darkies, this'd be a great place to bomb. A couple well-placed charges would bring down this flimsy rattrap like a cardhouse when you slam the front door.

Halfway through the song, Aames finally spotted the man he was looking for. Luther Hines was a prominent local black activist with eyes on a political future beyond the confines of New Orleans. Slim, impeccably dressed and well-groomed, his charismatic presence helped take an edge off the forcefulness of his rhetoric and countered allegations that he was merely a slicker version of his older brothers, Phil and George, who had been members of the Black Panther-linked National Committee to Combat Fascism. The Committee had been a militant group whose clash with police the previous decade had resulted in a bloody melee that had claimed one life and injured more than twenty.

Between numbers, Aames eased his way through the crowd and took a seat on the floor within earshot of Hines, who had come to the hall with a colleague several years older than him. It was difficult for Aames to catch much of the other men's conversation, but between songs the mercenary did manage to overhear that Hines planned to go straight home after he left the club, figuring he wanted a full night's sleep before the next day.

Hines lived alone in a renovated flat in the Lower Garden District, a few miles south of the French Quarter. U. D. Coates, another of Drago's men, had stood vigil outside the house earlier tonight, waiting for Hines to leave with his friend. By now, Aames figured Coates had had plenty of time to break in and get what Drago had sent him for. To make sure, when Hines got up to leave between sets, Aames hurried to the nearest pay phone and put through a quick call to yet another member of the crew, who was manning a cellular phone in an unmarked car parked down the block from Hines's address.

"He's on his way back," Aames reported.

"Alone?" the voice on the other end of the line asked.

Aames glanced over his shoulder and saw Hines shake hands with the friend before they parted company. Hines left while the other man returned to the main room of the hall. "Seems that way," Aames told his contact. "He said he was turning in early, so I don't think he's going to pick up any skirt on the way."

"Good."

Aames hung up and left the hall, lighting up another cigarillo the moment he was back out on the street. He looked at a clock mounted on a storefront across the street. A quarter past ten. He had more than an hour to kill before the guns were due. Plenty of time to track down his bookie and lay a bet on the Super Bowl.

STAN DRAGO FINISHED his beer while gazing at the smile of a sleek dancer spreading her legs for tips at the

Puss'n'Boots Club. She was naked and glistening with oil she'd spread over her body during the previous song. After she'd plucked Drago's dollar from the railing with a bit of anatomical prowess that earned whoops of disbelief from the other patrons, the dancer moved away from the mercenary and did a little shimmy-shake that would have made Jell-O envious. Drago winked at the woman and blew her a kiss. "Any time you need to take a breather from all that dancin', sweetheart, I'll keep you company," he told her.

"I'll remember that, hot rod," she laughed back at him, eyes on the bulge in his dungarees. "Maybe you'll let me drive that stick shift of yours, too, hmm?"

"Long as you know how to work it."

"Oh, I do, honey," she promised. "I'm good for all four gears and overdrive."

"How about reverse?"

The dancer turned her back to Drago and bent over at the waist, revealing a full moon above the mysterious forest that surrounded her magic pyramid. She peered out between her legs, face turned upside down. "Answer your question?"

"Hey, lady, something wrong with *our* money?" a potbellied insurance salesman on the other side of the stage complained, pointing a stubby finger at the dollar he'd set on the railing.

"Don't worry, pal, she'll get to you," Drago told the man. "Keep your pants on."

"He won't be able to when I'm through with him," the dancer teased as she worked her way across the stage. Looming over the salesman, she licked her lips and swayed to the disco beat emanating from a jukebox behind the stage. "Mister, you're about to break your britches...."

Drago left the stage area for a booth set far away from the action. He used a candle on the table to light a cigarette, and he blew smoke signals at a topless waitress hustling drinks a few booths away. She came over and let the candle's soft light play on her breasts.

"What can I get for you?" she asked pleasantly.

"Probably not what I want," Drago said, leering at the woman. "So make it a draft."

"Will do." The waitress had the good cheer of a flight attendant putting in her last shift before a pleasure cruise to Mazatlán. "Enjoy the show."

"I already have."

While he was waiting for his drink, Drago was joined by U. D. Coates, the shortest and wiriest member of his hellsquad, who paused a few seconds to ogle the stage show before slipping into the booth.

"Some prime poontang floatin' around here, eh, boss?"

Drago ignored the comment. His earlier grin had vanished, replaced by an icy cool. "What'd you manage to get?"

"I broke in with no problem," Coates prefaced as he went through his pockets and came up with a wadded handkerchief. He set it before Drago. "Here, take your pick."

Drago shielded the handkerchief with his forearm and used his free hand to unfold it, revealing a few small personal items belonging to Luther Hines. They included an admission pass to a local health club, a set of keys, a leather case holding a pair of prescription glasses and some political literature in various small pamphlets.

"Not bad, U.D.," he said, clumping the goods back up in the kerchief and pocketing them. "Not bad at all.

You're sure this is stuff he wouldn't miss right off, even the keys?''

Coates raised one hand as if he were on the witness stand. "Swear. They were stashed away in a bottom drawer with a ton of other crap."

"Good."

"He got home 'bout ten, fifteen minutes ago. Prob-ably's asleep by now."

Drago slipped out from his seat and set a five-dollar bill on the table. When the waitress showed up, he ges-tured at Coates. "Beer's for him."

"Oh." She seemed momentarily confused. "Leaving so soon?"

"Afraid so," Drago told her. "My mama always told me not to get spoiled by too much of a good thing."

"So lay those suds on me, sweetcakes," U.D. told the waitress, picking up the fiver and waving it like a mata-dor. *"Olé!"*

"I think you're supposed to be the one with the horns," the woman chuckled as she traded the beer for money. "Why don't you drink up and come ringside? I'm on next."

"Now you're talking!" Coates swilled his beer in one long swallow, then wiped his lips and headed for the stage as Drago strolled out into the New Orleans night.

He was on Bourbon Street, where the walk was lined with fast-talking hawkers pacing in front of garish en-tryways to other strip bars, touting the flesh shows going on inside. The street was crowded, mostly with normally straitlaced tourists indulging themselves with the closest they'd ever get to a walk on the wild side. Drago smirked as he saw a middle-aged man in an ill-fitting suit being reeled in by a hawker's spiel.

"C'mon, c'mon, step through these doors and you'll be in paradise. Six, count 'em, six lovelies every hour, each one a girl of your dreams, leaving nothing to the imagination. Just a small cover, friend. C'mon, c'mon. They're fine, they're foxy, and they all got a pretty little something just for you. Yes, you..."

Poor bastard, Drago mused. He'd be coming back out in an hour, horny as hell and poorer by thirty bucks that could have bought him ten minutes of the real thing with a streetwalker.

Not that Drago himself wasn't still tight in the groin from his visit to the Puss'n'Boots. But for him the arousal was strictly a preliminary to his real purpose for coming to the French Quarter this evening. He wanted to be charged up, primed for the one activity in his life that sex paled alongside.

It was killing time.

As he sauntered along with the flow of pedestrian traffic, Drago kept his eyes open for likely victims. There were plenty to choose from: people who reeked of vulnerability—timidness in their stride, a look of worried confusion on their faces, stopping under every second streetlight to pull out a map in hope of getting their bearings. After walking three blocks, he turned off Bourbon Street, following a couple in their mid-sixties who were overdressed, obviously lost, and from the look of it, a little drunk.

Perfect.

It didn't take long for the pedestrian traffic to thin out and for increasing darkness to take the place of the garish lighting that kept Bourbon Street in a constant state of illumination. Hookers similar to those who had seemed so charmingly inoffensive on the main strip now seemed to embody a greater evil, and shadowed figures hovering on doorsteps and in the alleyways took on a menacing aspect. The elderly couple drew closer together, and Drago could sense the fear in their whispered voices. He was walking less than twenty feet behind them, gaining ground with each step. They finally stopped beneath the nearest streetlight and turned to face Drago, terror in their eyes.

"Evening, folks," he told them, smiling. "You look like you're lost."

"W-we're trying to find Wilk Street," the woman stammered.

"You're a block off," Drago said. "I'm heading that way, though. If you'd like, I'll walk with you. It can get to be a little dangerous around here this time of night, especially if you're white. Know what I mean?"

The man nodded nervously, entwining arms with his wife as they proceeded alongside Drago and headed deeper into the darkness. Drago played tour guide, calming their fears with a patter of trivial observations about the area. All the while he scanned the neighborhood, looking for other signs of activity. Once he was sure that no one else was around, Drago took his right hand out of his coat pocket for the first time since he'd left the Puss'n'Boots. He was wearing a glove over the hand, and in that hand was a Ruger .22 target pistol, equipped with a silencer.

"Sorry, folks," he told the couple as he pulled the trigger twice. At this close range, Drago had no problems making sure both shots were lethal. The man and woman crumpled silently onto the sidewalk. Drago leaned over and grabbed both bodies, dragging them into a narrow alley that ran off the side street. It was pitch-dark in the passageway, and Drago hoped it would be dawn before the bodies were discovered.

Going back through his pockets, he took out the loaded handkerchief and shook its contents onto the pavement near the bodies.

"Hey, what the fuck you doin', dude?"

Drago spun around and saw a figure silhouetted in the entranceway to the alley. Acting on instinct, he whipped the Ruger into firing position and brought the intruder down with one quick shot to the chest.

It was a black youth in his midteens. Drago dragged him alongside the other bodies and fidgeted with various limbs to create the scenario he wanted cops to decide upon when they were called to the scene.

"You and Luther did these poor folks in, nigger boy," he told the bleeding teenager. "Only the old man put up a fight and you got in the way of a fluke shot. Tough break. And too bad ol' Luther didn't stick around to help."

15

"Me gusta la comida," Blancanales assured the waiter, leaning away from the table and patting his full stomach.

"¿Sí?"

"Sí." Pol pointed at what was left of his shrimp. *"Los camarónes."* He kissed his fingertips like an amateur gourmet trying to score points with Julia Child.

The waiter turned to Lyons and raised his eyebrows questioningly. *"¿Señor?* Your food is good, too?"

Lyons nodded, his mouth still full of lobster. "Whatever he said goes double for me," he said between bites, indicating Blancanales.

"La cuenta," Pol said, writing in the air with an imaginary pen.

"Un momento." As the waiter went off to add up the check, Mike Armstrong dabbed his lips with his napkin, then shook his head at Blancanales.

"This one's on me, boys."

"No way," Pol said. "Hal wouldn't hear of it."

"Well, since you put it that way, I'd be a fool to—"

Mike was interrupted by a high-pitched beep emanating from his midsection. He reached for his belt and snapped off a clip-on beeper.

"A pager?" Blancanales said. "Since when did you have a staff working for you?"

"Since I married Sarah twenty-four years ago," Mike said as he slid away from the booth. "She likes to keep one ear on the shortwave at night when I'm out on the prowl. Excuse me a sec, okay?"

The waiter returned with the check as Mike left to use the phone. Blancanales raided his wallet for some of his allotted petty cash and regarded Lyons, who was staring into what was left of his bourbon. "Town's really got you down, eh, mon?"

Lyons stared back at his friend. "Kinda stirs things up a little, that's all."

"Gotta expect that, I guess. You know, maybe you shoulda stayed up in Birmingham and let Gadgets—"

"No way," Lyons insisted. "Look, Pol, you know I'm not the type to duck the hard road. I'll be okay, especially once I get a chance to take this funk out on some more of those Klan clones."

"That's the spirit, Ironman. Nut up and do it."

"Amen."

Armstrong returned to the booth and grabbed his Stetson from the table without bothering to sit down. "Appears our timetable's a little off kilter," he told the other men. "Sarah says the cops just got tipped off to the arms drop. It's going down tonight."

"Tonight?" Adrenaline was already evicting the negligible traces of alcohol in Lyons's system.

"Seems so. Some ARC punk just came down with a case of conscience and called the station."

"Legit?"

"Can't say for sure until they check it out," Armstrong admitted. "But they quizzed the guy about some confidential stuff they have on Drago's outfit, and his answers all checked out."

Pol slid out of the booth, followed by Lyons. As the three of them headed for the door, Blancanales asked, "The waterfront?"

Armstrong nodded. "I hope you boys brought your swim trunks...."

As WITH MOST DELTA AREAS around the globe, one of the most ongoing threats to the waterways of New Orleans was the buildup of silt deposits that, if left unchecked, could eventually choke off access to the docks. Accordingly it was not uncommon to find any number of huge, lumbering dredges out near the mouth of the Mississippi River, outriggings of linked pontoons trailing behind them in wide sweeping arcs to mark where underwater scoops were scraping the river bottom.

One such dredge was moored for the night a few dozen yards out into the river near a run-down section of the city's sprawling wharfline. The crew had punched out at sundown, but a security guard remained on board to keep vandals and teenage thrill seekers from seeking out the craft as a possible site for misadventure. He was an older man with a hefty paunch and antiquated muttonchops that seemed to be attached to the wire-rimmed frames of his bifocals. Normally he spent most of his night shift in the pilot's cabin, reading by lamplight with the window partially opened so that he could hear any suspicious sounds. Old though he was, the geezer had a good set of ears and enough experience on the water to detect and discern noises that would have been lost on landlubbers.

Tonight, however, the guard had the window closed and the shade lowered. Instead of a book, he had the television on, turned up loud. A professional wrestler who'd played the circuit as Muskrat Pete in his earlier days, the man cheered along to the flickering images of late-night wrestling on the screen, letting himself get caught up in the action. There was no way he'd be able to hear anything going on outside the pilot's cabin. An old acquaintance by the name of Stan Drago had paid him handsomely to look the other way tonight, and Muskrat Pete knew just enough about Drago to realize it was in his best interests to keep his end of the bargain.

While Muskrat Pete immersed himself in the antics of Hulk Hogan and the Junkyard Dog, a twenty-foot-long Chris-Craft cut its engines and floated to a stop near the port side of the idle dredge. The cabin cruiser's lights went out, and only the faint glow of cigarettes betrayed the positions of the five men on deck. In the background, by contrast, the city glittered with nightlife, and Plaza Tower rose forty-five stories into the hazy aura that covered New Orleans like a dome.

Elsewhere up and down the river, there would be considerable activity even at this late hour, but here the waters were quiet save for the lapping of the current against dock pilings and against the hulls of the dredge and cabin cruiser.

Then, off near the blackness of a supposedly deserted boathouse, an outboard motor sputtered into life. Moments later a low-lying boat roamed out into the river, leaving a triangular wake as it cut across the current on its way to the larger cruiser. Rob Aames manned the Evinrude, keeping it as quiet as possible as he steered. A Belgian FN rested on his lap. U. D. Coates had a similar rifle in his hands up at the front of the small craft. Drago sat between them, money in his coat pocket, a Smith & Wesson Model 581 revolver in his right hand. Until he had a chance to master use of the Grossler Stealth-shooter, the Smith & Wesson would remain his handgun of choice. Loaded with Remington 158-grain Soft Points, it was an instrument of powerful persuasion, if a little loud and obnoxious when having its say.

Coates flicked a small penlight in a coded sequence and was answered by a series of flickers from the deck of the cabin cruiser. A rope ladder clattered down the craft's side as the motorboat pulled alongside it.

"Leave the engine running," Drago told Aames as he stood up and reached for the ladder. "I don't aim on this taking too long. U.D., you get the honors."

Coates edged past Drago and started up the ladder. Two dark figures appeared near the top of the ladder, ready to give U.D. a lift aboard.

"Move aside, gents," he told the strangers. "I can take care of myself."

"Suit yourself," one of the deckhands replied, snapping his cigarette over the side as he and his cohort moved away from the ladder. Coates joined them on the deck, still toting his rifle. Drago followed.

"Hey, Abner," he told the skipper of the larger boat, a tall man missing half the fingers of his left hand as a result of poor judgment during a poker game years ago. "You have any problems?"

Abner Smith shook his head. "Chopper showed up right on the money. Speaking of which..."

"Don't worry, I've got the cash," Drago assured the other man. His eyes fell on the parcels resting on the deck between them. The protective padding had already been removed, and the crate lids had also been loosened. "They all there?"

"By my count they are," Smith said.

"Not that I don't trust you, Abner..." Drago crouched before the crates and pulled off one of the lids. Moonlight shone off the polished metal of the packed Stealth-shooters and boxes of ammunition. Drago shifted his

Smith & Wesson to his left hand so he could pick up one of the semiautomatics with his right. Coates aimed the penlight Drago's way so that they could have a better look at the weapon.

"Looks pretty slick to me," Coates said.

"Yeah, it does. Now if they only work . . ."

Drago heard an unmistakable click and glanced up into the business end of Abner's .44 Magnum Virginian Dragoon, a nasty-looking revolver with a six-inch barrel. Behind Smith, Drago saw that the skipper's flunkies were armed with Remington 572 pump rifles.

"Hope you didn't figure on sampling the merchandise here," Abner drawled lazily.

"That's not what I meant," Drago said, keeping his eyes on the weapons aimed at him and Coates. "Ease up, Abner."

"I'll ease up once we're squared away and you're outta here," Smith said. "Look, I fronted payment for these cap pistols because I owed you a favor. All you gotta do is reimburse me and everything's cool."

Drago sighed and carefully set the Stealthshooter back in its crate. He'd considered double-crossing Smith and trying to come away from the transaction with not only the guns but also with Abner's prized speedboat, which would have been a nice addition to ARC's holdings. But obviously Smith knew him too well and was prepared for any attempts at foul play. Drago stood slowly and reached for the envelope with Stevens's cash in it.

"You disappoint me, Abner," he said. "Old friends like us, carrying on like this . . ."

A blinding shaft of light suddenly cut through the river air, startling all the men on both boats. Drago blocked the glare with his palm as he looked toward shore.

"Police!" came the call from the docks. Rooftop bea-
cons began to flash from no less than seven patrol cars
spaced out along the wharves, and more searchlights cast
their focused brilliance on the Chris-Craft. "You're all
under arrest!"

Drago shook off his surprise and snapped into action.
Bringing his Smith & Wesson up into a two-handed firing stance, he squeezed the trigger twice. His second shot
took out the first spotlight. Abner's men followed
Drago's cue and vented their Remingtons at the other
squad cars, trying to return darkness to the area. The
police began returning fire, and bullets scarred the cabin
cruiser.

"Shit!" Smith ducked for cover. "Bad enough I have
to deal with you, Drago! This I don't need."

"Quit yer bitchin' and get this tub rolling!" Drago
snapped back as he peered over the gunwale and emptied another round from his Smith & Wesson.

"SOUNDS LIKE THEY STARTED the party without us,"
Lyons said as the sound of gunfire reverberated along the
wharves.

He was riding shotgun next to Mike Armstrong, who
drove his Chevy sedan through the darkened back streets
that ran behind the docks. Blancanales was in the back
seat, readying a pair of Kissinger-modified M-16s for
action. Glancing out at the blur of dilapidated buildings
Armstrong was passing, he remarked, "Reminds me of
that pirate ride at Disneyland."

"Well, this isn't Disneyland, and it sure as hell isn't the
Caribbean," Armstrong countered as he made one last
sharp turn and brought the Chevy to an abrupt stop
along the docks. The private investigator snapped off his
lights, but not before giving away their position to the

enemy out on the water. A blast of rifle fire slammed loudly into a front quarterpanel, jarring the whole vehicle.

"And they aren't firing blanks, either." Lyons snatched one of the M-16s from Pol and switched it onto autoburn as he jerked his door open and rolled out.

They were nearly a hundred yards north of where the police had arrived on the scene. Shots were still being traded between the cops and the men aboard the speedboat. Lyons quickly surmised that the blast that had greeted them had come from a closer distance, and as his eyes quickly adjusted themselves to the relative darkness of the water, he spotted the smaller motorboat Rob Aames was trying to escape in. The mercenary had just set down his rifle in favor of the rudder and controls of the Evinrude.

"Shouldn't have wasted time on that potshot, pal," Lyons advised the boatman as he fired his M-16. The rifle rocked and rolled in his grip as it sprayed a volley of hot lead at the fleeing boat.

Aames took four direct hits, three in the upper body and one in the head. What was left of him slumped over the outboard motor, turning the rudder sharply to one side so that the boat began to chug about in a tight circle that would inevitably bring it crashing into the docks.

"Well, trunks or not . . ."

Lyons passed his M-16 to Armstrong and broke into a run toward the edge of the wharf, at the last second springing forward so that he dived cleanly into the cold, brackish waters of the Mississippi. By the time he came up for air, he was already halfway to the errant motorboat.

BLANCANALES AND ARMSTRONG ADVANCED in the darkness of the wharves toward where the police were stationed. As they drew closer, they realized that the authorities had to contend with additional gunmen besides those based on the larger speedboat, whose engines were just now throbbing back into life next to the barge. Drago had stationed four of his men to guard the docks during the gun exchange, and they were now emptying their Belgian FNs at the cops from the cover of an old rusting forklift and a five-foot-high stack of skids. The police, caught up in a partial cross fire, lost three men in a matter of seconds, and the others had to stop firing as they scrambled for better cover.

Armstrong knew that the M-16 Lyons had given him was already on full automatic. Blancanales chose the same option for his rifle, and they fell into firing crouches before letting loose on the landbound mercenaries. Unfortunately Lyons's earlier shots had tipped off their position, and Drago's men weren't taken by surprise when Pol and Armstrong fired. Hollowpoints chewed at the wooden slats of the skids and raised sparks when they glanced off the metallic hide of the forklift, but none of the bullets found flesh.

When ARC riflemen returned fire, Armstrong and Blancanales dived in opposite directions to avoid the horizontal rain. Blancanales rammed his shoulder against an iron mooring post but had little time to notice any pain before he felt a hot zip of agony shoot up his right leg. Even before he had a chance to look, he knew he'd been hit. Blood soaked through his gray pants just above the knee.

"Bastards!" He threw in a quick torrent of expletives in his native Spanish as he tried to ignore the pain and concentrate on the four figures he saw breaking from

cover fifty yards away. They were headed for an alley that
separated run-down shacks on the wharf. Between him
and Armstrong, their second volley proved more successful, bringing down one of the men. However, by the
time Pol limped to catch up with the older man near the
alley, they both could hear the squeal of tires and see the
taillights of the retreating car.

"Shit," Pol muttered.

"You're bleeding, friend," Armstrong told him.

"Yeah," Blancanales grumbled, "and I just bought
these pants last week."

LYONS PULLED himself aboard the small boat, no easy
feat given its circling course. His fingertips were numb
from the icy water, and he shivered involuntarily as he
made his way to the back of the craft and pitched Aames
over the side. Freed of the dead man's weight, the motor
shifted and started propelling the boat directly toward the
docks. Lyons quickly steered wide of the pilings and
opened the throttle as he aimed the boat's prow at the
dredge.

The cabin cruiser was in motion now, pulling away
from the dredge. Men aboard the craft continued to fire
at the police on the docks, and when Muskrat Pete made
the mistake of venturing too close to the window of the
dredge's pilot cabin, he learned there was great truth in
the parable that curiosity killed the cat. A stray shower
of bullets peppered the cabin window, and he tumbled
out through the shattered glass, fatally perforated even
before he landed headfirst against the dredge's iron railing and splashed lifelessly into the river.

Finding Aames's abandoned Belgian FN too cumber-
some to fire while he was trying to run the boat, Lyons
reached into his drenched shoulder holster for his Gov-

ernment Model .45. Although the weapon wasn't meant to be slogged through water, Kissinger's customizing talents had taken weatherproofing into consideration, and when he took one-handed aim at the approaching cruiser and pulled the trigger, the gun fired. Wide of the mark, but it fired.

Rounding the dredge, the larger boat continued to pick up speed, and within seconds Lyons realized that whoever was at the helm was aiming for him. With the network of the dredge's pontoons blocking his way to the right, his only free course was a sharp left, which would only put him out into the middle of the river where he'd be an even easier target for the other vessel to hit. He'd blundered his way into the nautical equivalent of being between a rock and a hard place.

A second shot from his .45 kissed harmlessly off the siding of the cabin cruiser, which loomed closer and closer like a hungry fish about to jump on a slower minnow. Lyons briefly gambled on a third course of action and guided his boat toward a direct collision course with its larger counterpart.

"Chicken of the seas," he found himself whispering.

Twenty yards separated the two boats. Aboard the Chris-Craft, Stan Drago stopped firing at the shore cops and leveled his newly acquired Stealthshooter at Lyons. There was no discernible sound as the trigger was pulled, and the Ironman caught only the faintest and briefest glint of a flash before bullets were glancing off the side of the motorboat.

Fifteen yards.

Lyons ducked sharply to one side as the bullets stitched past him and clanged off the Evinrude's casing without damaging the motor. Somehow the Ironman managed to keep his hand on the rudder.

Ten yards.

Nine . . . eight . . . seven . . .

When the cabin cruiser was only six yards away from turning Lyons's craft into kindling, he veered sharply to his right and let his reflexes take over. With a splintering crash, the boat slammed into one of the pontoons at nearly full speed. Lyons was hurled forward, head over heels, losing his .45 as his airborne flight carried him just over the top of an adjacent pontoon. He hit the water with considerably less grace than his earlier dive, and the force of impact knocked the wind from his lungs.

BLANCANALES AND ARMSTRONG JOINED the police who hadn't driven off to give chase to the mercenaries fleeing by car. When Pol saw the motorboat shatter against the pontoon, he broke away from the others.

"Wait!" Armstrong called out after him. "Your leg!"

But a bullet wound in the leg was the last thing on Pol's mind, although he did limp noticeably as he cleared the distance to the water's edge. He waited long enough to take aim and fire off one last burst at the retreating speedboat, nailing one of the gunmen aboard, then lowered himself to the pontoons, which were connected at spaced intervals by flat, narrow planks. Wet and lined with moss, the planks offered poor footing, but Blancanales had been forced to traverse far worse surfaces in the line of duty. He made his way from pontoon to pontoon, eyes on the dark waters off to his right.

"Ironman!" he called out. "Hey, buddy, I'm coming!"

The gunfire had subsided, replaced by the sound of sirens wailing in the distance. A police chopper hovered over the scene, and downriver a pair of Coast Guard ships came into view, one giving chase to the long-gone speedboat while the other droned its way toward the dredge. Just beyond the ravaged pontoon Lyons had collided with, Blancanales spotted his partner floating facedown in the water. A sharp jabbing pain once again ran the length of Pol's leg as he pushed off the planks and dived into the water, swimming after the inert form of Lyons. When he reach the other man, Blancanales carefully flipped him over, mindful of possible neck injuries, then secured a lifesaver's grip that kept the unconscious victim's head above the shallow waves as he used his free arm to stroke their way back to the nearest pontoon. Mike Armstrong and one of the local cops had come out to lend assistance, and they helped drag Lyons up out of the water.

"He's still got a pulse," Blancanales gasped as he pulled himself up onto the planks.

Lyons stirred slightly when Armstrong shifted him into position for artificial resuscitation. With a loud, hacking cough, the Ironman spat up a mouthful of water and opened his eyes. His vision was clouded momentarily, but when the triplicate images before him narrowed down to one, he saw Blancanales leaning over him, grinning.

"Hey, *amigo*, you look a little green around the gills."

Lyons managed a smirk. "My mother always told me I shouldn't go swimming right after I ate...."

16

Cowboy Kissinger passed through security clearance and entered his temporary workshop in the Birmingham FBI building. Gadgets Schwarz was standing near the bench, examining several in-depth schematic diagrams laid out next to the FOG-M missile system.

"What do you make of it?" Kissinger asked as he opened the brown bag he was carrying and pulled out a pair of submarine sandwiches. The two men had been holed up in the workshop all morning, putting their heads together with the hope that their combined knowledge might turn up some constructive ideas for modifying the missile for use by Able Team.

"I have to say that whoever they had putting this baby together knew what he was doing." Gadgets tapped the diagrams and shook his head admiringly. "Hardly any excess fat at all. I've got a few ideas for beefing up the computer efficiency, but that's not going to make it lighter by any more than a few ounces."

Kissinger handed one of the sandwiches to Schwarz and unwrapped the other one for himself. "That makes it unanimous," he conceded. "It'd be nice if it could be made a little more portable, but it could still come in handy the way it is. Price is right, too. I think I'll have Brognola get us a couple more."

They ate quietly for a few moments before the door opened and Agent Coe entered the room. No one was going to mistake him for the Good Humor man.

"Bad news?" Gadgets asked through a mouthful of pastrami and provolone.

"It isn't good."

The FBI operative went on to explain about the shootout at the docks in New Orleans and the injuries sustained by Blancanales and Lyons. "They're both taped up and tired as hell, but Lyons says they'll be ready to pick up where they left off in another day," he concluded.

"What about ARC? How many of theirs did we get?"

"Two dead, one in a coma," Coe replied. "The rest slipped through the cracks before a dragnet could be set up. I imagine there's a full force out looking for 'em today."

"It won't be a full force till we get there," Schwarz said. He took another bite from his sandwich and wrapped the rest back up. "Think you can get us down there in a hurry?"

"I'll do the best I can," Coe promised, "but if you're gonna be hauling your hardware again we have to keep you off the commercial flyers. It'll take a couple hours to line something up."

SIX HOURS WAS MORE LIKE IT.

The sun had just gone down by the time Kissinger and Schwarz deplaned from a private jet at New Orleans International and were hustled into an unmarked FBI sedan that took them to the hotel room in the French Quarter where Blancanales and Lyons were recuperating. Pol's thigh was tightly bound to prevent infection in what turned out to be a come-and-go gunshot wound—

the bullet had been kind enough to avoid any vital organs on its brief tour through his body. Lyons had four cracked ribs and more bruises than the last piece of fruit in a produce bin.

"Hey, guys," Schwarz told them, "I already know I'm indispensable to the Team. You didn't have to go through all this to prove it."

Blancanales gave Gadgets a one-finger salute. "Don't flatter yourself, Schwarz," Lyons told him. He tried to keep a straight face, but his jaw was too sore to remain clenched.

Kissinger had picked up an edition of the evening paper, and as he skimmed the headlines he commented, "Lot going on here last night. You guys barely made the front page."

Of course, as far as the general public was concerned, Lyons and Blancanales were lumped in with law-enforcement casualties and no mention was made of their affiliation with Stony Man Farm. For that matter, the entire incident at the docks had been downplayed as just another installment in an ongoing series of battles between smugglers and the law that dated back to the eighteenth century.

The bulk of the front-page headlines was devoted to the murder of two elderly white tourists on a side street only a few blocks from the heart of the French Quarter. Based on evidence found at the scene, police had arrested local black activist Luther Hines as an alleged accessory to the crime, which purportedly had been committed by a sixteen-year-old black youth. The youth had died while on his way to a nearby hospital, apparently having been shot by his own gun during a struggle with the murder victims. Based on Hines's family connections with the supposedly defunct black militant

National Committee to Combat Fascism and the fact that
NCCF pamphlets had been found near the bodies, police were advancing a theory that the killings may have
been in retaliation for the earlier mass murders of black
families in Birmingham. In other related stories, it was
reported that racial tension, not only in New Orleans but
throughout the South, had reached a level unmatched
since the early sixties. A number of isolated incidents over
the past few weeks pointed to a disturbing pattern of violence that would only be reinforced by this most recent
set of killings in the French Quarter.

"There seems to be a hell of a lot of coincidence going
on here," Lyons said after Kissinger had passed him the
paper and he'd had a chance to look it over. "First, this
nutcase in Birmingham turns out to be using the same
kind of gun that's being shipped to ARC down here, then
we get more murders taking place a couple of miles from
where they pick up their shipment."

"I don't like the way it adds up, either," Schwarz said.
He looked over at Kissinger. "Was this Crosley guy ever
tied up in any racist shit back in Wisconsin?"

"Not that I knew about, obviously," Cowboy told
him. "Of course, it turns out he had me in the dark about
a lot of things, so I wouldn't count it out."

An inside doorway linked the room with a common
bathroom all four men would be sharing. As Kissinger
hauled his luggage into the adjacent suite, Schwarz stayed
behind with his cohorts. "What's our next move?"

Lyons yawned, wincing at the pain that mere gesture
brought him. "Armstrong's got clearance through
Brognola to stay on top of what the locals come up with
as far as tracking down Drago. He'll call here if they
make any headway. They're hoping to get another call
from the snitch who tipped them off to the gun ship-

ment, but that seems like a long shot. If you guys want to chip in, I'm sure they can plug you in somewhere. As for me, I'll be a whole lot more useful once these bruises calm down and I get the cobwebs out of my skull.''

"Might be good if we all get a good chunk of shut-eye under our belts," Schwarz said. "Flying in here I saw a lot of swampland these shits could have fled to. Let's let the bloodhounds narrow things down for us."

"You got my vote on that," Blancanales said, carefully swinging his bad leg up onto the bed. "I tell you, me and the Ironman were both up all last night at the hospital. Nurses there aren't happy unless they can yank you out of dreamland once an hour for one damn reason or another."

"Ain't that the truth," Lyons agreed. "We finally had to check out and tell 'em we'd take two aspirin and call 'em in the morning."

Gadgets left his companions and headed off to the other room, where Kissinger was just wrapping up a call to headquarters.

"Yeah, well thanks for passing that along, chief," Cowboy said. "Be talking to you soon." He slowly hung up the receiver and stared into space, unaware at first that Schwarz had joined him.

"What's the word?" Gadgets asked.

"Turns out ARC isn't the only group doing business with Crosley," Kissinger explained. "Brognola got calls from agents in New York and Lebanon. Both have turned up the same rumor that Shiites have cut a deal for a few hundred QA-18s."

"Ouch," Schwarz grimaced at the news. "Small world."

"And getting smaller every day."

Gadgets sat on the edge of his bed and massaged a kink on the back of his neck. "You thinking what I'm thinking, Cowboy?"

Kissinger nodded. "Somehow all this shit's coming from the same toilet."

Gadgets kicked off his shoes and lay back on the hard mattress. As he stared at the ceiling, he murmured, "I just hope we're the ones that get to flush it."

17

The sun rose through the mist above Plaquemines Parish. Geese honked in formation as they flew over the heads of Stan Drago and his dozing counterparts. The commander sat upright, shaking off his dreams, instantly alert to his surroundings, Smith & Wesson in hand.

They were in one of ARC's several bayou field quarters, a sunken concrete cell elaborately concealed from casual view by the half-flattened barn they'd painstakingly built under. Sparsely furnished because of the need for quick evacuation during the flood season, the chamber reeked of mildew and sweat. Beams of light worked their way through gaps in the barn wall and fell on the faces of the other men.

"All right, snap to," Drago ordered as he rose from his cot. He'd chosen this particular cell for their hideout because it was the only one that hadn't been used during the time that Louis Billingsworth had been with ARC. Louis had disappeared the previous night after excusing himself to take a leak shortly before the incident near the dredge, and it was assumed that he was the one who had tipped off the police about the pending gun shipment. Drago wasn't about to go near any of the other compounds for fear that Billingsworth had already divulged their whereabouts.

Abner Smith was on the cot next to Drago. He sat up, sullen-faced, Dragoon revolver still in his hand like an extension of his fingers, and directed his foul mood at the ARC leader. "Maybe I don't have any choice but to string along for the time being, but I'll be goddamned if I'm gonna play buck private for you."

Drago had to make a quick decision. He'd lost a few good men last night and had hoped that Smith and his sidekicks might prove to be adequate substitutes, at least long enough to carry out their mission. But already the other man was questioning his authority, and he could sense that Abner's three surviving cohorts would side with their skipper if push came to shove. Even his own men's interest in the altercation seemed to be from a position of less than total allegiance. Just my fucking luck, Drago thought to himself.

"Tell you what, Abner," Drago bartered. "There's nine of us and five of you, so if you want to call me on, let's go for it right now and be done with it."

As Drago expected, Smith hesitated, doing his best to keep a poker face. "I'm just saying we can get through this as partners instead of pulling all this rank crap, *capiche*?"

"Sounds fair by me," Drago said. "Look, we're already squared away on the guns. Everyone gets equal shares when we get paid for today, okay?"

"Maybe," Abner replied casually. "You still haven't said what it is you've got in mind as far as today goes."

Drago lit a cigarette and blew smoke at the rafters before replying. "I'll let you know about that when the time's right."

"No good. I want to know now."

"Abner, Abner, Abner..." Drago turned away from the skipper and shook his head ruefully, at the same time taking in his men with a short, sweeping gaze. Well, he thought, it's gotta happen, one way or another. Almost as an afterthought, he turned back and flicked his cigarette Smith's way. The skipper was distracted momentarily, and a moment was all Drago needed.

With lightning speed, he lunged forward, in the same motion using his free hand to pull his hunting knife free of its sheath. The blade ripped up through Abner's shirt and the soft flesh beneath his ribs, then twisted its way to the man's heart. Blood gushed warmly down the knife's hilt and onto Drago's fingers as his other hand expertly jabbed at a pressure point on the underside of Smith's wrist, ensuring that the Dragoon revolver clattered to the floor without the dead man's final reflexes getting off a shot.

"You dumb fuck," Drago hissed into Abner's lifeless eyes as he pinned the body against the nearest wall. "Couldn't take orders for a few fucking hours, could you?"

Behind Drago, his men quickly surrounded Smith's followers, some of them using Belgian FNs, others the new Stealthshooters. Outnumbered, the second group took the hint and dropped their own weapons.

Drago stepped away from Abner and let the body fall to the concrete. He reached past the flowing blood for the envelope filled with the cash he'd given Smith for the shipment of guns. After wiping his hands off on a stray rag, he took the money out and carefully counted it in front of the prisoners.

"Okay, boys, now it's your turn." He stood before Abner's men and slipped an equal share of the currency into each of their pockets. "You want to earn the right to spend that, or do we practice some more open-heart surgery?"

Drago hadn't bothered to clean his hunting knife, and he let the prisoners have a good look at its bloodstained blade. After what amounted to a little more than a token pause, the oldest of the four men spoke on behalf of the others.

"What you got in mind, boss?"

Drago grinned and slowly wiped the knife clean. "That's what I like to hear," he said, squatting down on his haunches and gesturing for the others to huddle around him as he scrawled a diagram on the muddy floor. "Last night was kiddie's play compared to what's going down today. The first thing we're all going to do is make sure we know how to use these zip guns, then we're going to take a little trip down to a bend in the river and wait to throw a surprise party for a guy named Hobst. Maybe you know him?"

18

A tuba woke Blancanales from a dream that had him tap-dancing on the pontoons of a river dredge while an unseen foe shot bullets at his feet like some villain out of a B-western. As he stirred in bed, painfully aware of the dull throb in his wounded thigh, trumpets, drums and saxophones joined the tuba in a slow, mournful dirge.

In the other bed, Lyons was already up, ear cocked toward their second-story window. "You hear that?" he asked Blancanales.

"*Sí.*"

"Good." Lyons swung his legs to the floor and slowly stood up. "Then I just *feel* hung over. I tell ya, Pol, no more demolition derbies for this kid."

There was a light rap of knuckles on the bathroom door. Schwarz poked his head into their room. "We ordered up some breakfast if you're interested."

"Ah, food!" Blancanales perked up, grabbing for his clothes at the foot of the bed.

"I feel like my belly's still black and blue," Lyons said, "but maybe once I get some java in the crankcase my pistons might kick in."

"That's the spirit." Pol stepped into his pants and padded barefoot to the window, parting the shades for a look at the street below. Two blocks away, a brass band was leading a funeral procession along the wide sidewalk. The players were black, as were most of the mourners. "Just a Closer Walk with Thee" was the song, and it stirred up faint memories of Blancanales's youth in East Los Angeles, where his barrio had bordered a black neighborhood and a church where rousing spirituals often spilled out into the streets on Saturday nights and on Sundays.

"Must be for that kid that died the other night," he said as he stepped back from the window and put on a shirt.

"Sounds like quite a send-off for an alleged murderer," Lyons reflected.

"Well, there's more than well-wishers down there," Blancanales observed.

Lyons joined his partner near the window and took in the procession. At various spots along the streets, clots of angry whites were gathered, trying to drown out the brass band with racial taunts.

"Niggers!"

"Hang the body!"

"March back to Africa, jigaboos!"

When a hurled stick struck one of the band members, some of the marchers broke away from the procession to confront the protestors. Words, then punches were traded, triggering a brawl that seemed destined to spread throughout the block until police officers converged on the scene, some on horseback and the rest on foot, determined to restore order.

"I don't like what I'm seeing." Blancanales moved away from the window to finish dressing. "This is taking me back to '67, and that wasn't a good year."

"Watts?"

Pol nodded. "Watts got most of the headlines, but a lot of shit went down in the barrio, too. An ugly scene, homes. A real ugly scene."

"I know what you mean," Lyons said. "I felt trouble brewing back in Birmingham, too. Read between the lines of what some of the politicians down here are peddling and it's Lester Maddox all over again, just a little more sugarcoated." He slapped on a shoulder holster carrying his old standby Colt Python. The .45 he'd used against the gun smugglers was now on the bottom of the Mississippi River. As they started for the other room, Lyons punched Blancanales lightly on the shoulder. "By the way, thanks again for fishing me out the other night."

"You would have done the same for me, right?"

"True, but still . . . tell you what. No more wisecracks about your chili from me, how's that?"

Blancanales laughed and held out his hand. "I'm gonna need a handshake on that one."

"Deal," Lyons said, pumping his friend's hand. "Now let's go grab us some grits."

Besides grits, Schwarz had ordered up two pots of coffee, steak and eggs, oyster loaf poor boys and *muffuletta*, a monstrous sandwich piled high with ham, salami, mozzarella and provolone. The entire room was rich with the mingling aromas, and Blancanales rubbed his palms together as he eyed the offerings. "Robbed a restaurant for all this, Gadgets?" he said.

"Beats whatever they gave you at the hospital, I'll bet," Schwarz said. "Dig in while it's hot."

"Try to stop me."

Kissinger was off in the corner, cleaning the weapons that had been used in the other night's firestorm. "I'm sure it breaks your heart having to fall back on that Python," he told Lyons, raising his voice to be heard above the brass band that was now passing directly below their window.

Lyons patted the stock of his holstered weapon. "Yeah, I'm all shook up about it."

"I'll bet." It was only recently that Lyons and his cohorts had begun to carry .45s, bending to Kissinger's logic that sharing the same type of ammunition could be a lifesaving consideration in the thick of battle. But, just as Schwarz always had his silenced 93-R tucked away nearby and Pol was always eager for an excuse to fall back on his M-203 combo, the Ironman subscribed to the American Express Card philosophy when it came to his personal fave—he didn't leave home without it.

"Only thing the locals came up with so far was the getaway car," Schwarz said, briefing Pol and Lyons as they loaded their plates with food. "It was stolen, of course. There's a search going on out in the bayou country, but that's even more ground to cover than we had to worry about back in Birmingham."

Lyons bit into a poor boy and gave a grunt of satisfaction as his tastebuds caught up with his sense of smell. After washing down the bread with coffee, he said, "No word on the boat, either? Man, that was the biggest damn cabin cruiser I ever saw."

"That might have had something to do with your perspective, Ironman," Blancanales kidded.

"Maybe so, but I still think that..." Lyons's voice faded as he looked in the direction of the window. He put a finger to his lips and jerked the Python .357 from his holster. The others could hear it now, too—the sound of someone apparently using the band's racket to mask an attempt to gain access to the room's terrace.

Although in some respects the Colt was an inferior weapon to the .45, its six-inch barrel was still a deadly sight, likely to convince whoever was on the other side of the window that he had picked the wrong time and place to dabble in burglary. Lyons took a short breath, then swung the gun into firing position as Kissinger sharply pulled aside the shades.

"Don't shoot!"

A ten-year-old boy trembled on the terrace, his dark hands raised above his head. There was fear in his eyes. "Please don't shoot," he repeated.

Lyons kept his gun at the ready and opened the window. "What the hell are you doing out there?" he demanded.

"Mr. Armstrong told me to see you," the youth said. "It's important."

"Armstrong sent you?"

"Yes, sir."

Lyons looked past the boy at the wrought-iron grillwork that rose from the street in front of this and nearly every other building on the block. The funeral march was just turning around the corner. The Ironman turned back to the lad. "You ever heard of using a door?"

"I tried, but the man in the lobby chased me out." The youth looked hard at the man with the gun before asking, "Are you Mr. Lyons?"

The boy was wearing tight shorts and T-shirt, and in a glance Lyons could see he wasn't armed. Nodding, he lowered his gun and helped the boy inside. The phone rang, and Schwarz answered it.

"'lo...oh, hi, Armstrong. Funny you should call." As he listened to the man on the other end of the line, Schwarz looked at the uninvited guest. "Yeah, he just showed up here. Oh, yeah? Yeah, sure. We'll do what we can. Talk to you later."

"Checks out?" Blancanales asked.

Gadgets nodded. "Guys, this is Jimmy Spencer. His brother's the one they're on their way to bury."

"He got shot a couple of nights ago," Jimmy said matter-of-factly. "I found him and called the cops."

"I see," Lyons said. "And why did Mr. Armstrong want you to come to us?"

A single tear worked its way down Jimmy's cheek. "My brother was still alive when I found him."

Lyons traded glances with the other men, then looked back at Jimmy. "Did he say anything?"

Jimmy nodded. "He said a white guy shot him."

STAN DRAGO STOOD near a bend in the river where great willows rose from the shoreline and swayed like hoop-skirts in the breeze. He seemed to be alone on the embankment, smoking contentedly like a cigarette poster boy on a location shoot. Far to the north, the higher buildings of New Orleans were barely visible above the horizon.

"This should do," he mumbled to himself. Of course, the site had been on his mind since Stevens had first propositioned him regarding the elimination of Governor Hobst. As someone who had spent the better part of seven years frequenting this last stretch of the Mississippi before it met the Gulf of Mexico, Drago was in his element here. He knew how much water traffic could be expected, how fast any range of boats could effectively travel when taking the sharp, snag-choked bend in the river and, most importantly, escape routes he and his men could take after they'd struck.

It was common for the river to carry along bits of driftwood or other debris in its current, and when Drago spotted a particularly large log floating slowly toward the bend, he dropped his cigarette in the mud and headed off into the tawny, waist-high marsh grass that grew all the way to the water's edge.

"All right, everyone!" he called out. We're going after the big log coming downstream. On my signal..."

Switching off the safety on his Stealthshooter, Drago made his way to a recessed cove where Abner's cabin cruiser was moored, hidden from view beneath the willows. Drago took aim over its softly bobbing deck, waiting for the log to drift into view.

"Now!"

On both sides of the river, men armed with the silencer-equipped automatics rose into view, heads and shoulders above the grass as they fired at their floating target.

Making no more noise than blowguns in an aborigine ambush, the Stealthshooters chipped away at the log and pelted the surrounding water with whizzing 9 mm rounds and bark shrapnel. Inside of five seconds, the log took a cross fire of more than three dozen direct hits and was proportionately whittled down in size.

"Any misfires?" Drago called out. From his position he could see the other men shake their heads. U. D. Coates flashed a thumbs-up signal and quickly reloaded his Grossler so that he could get off another fifteen shots at the retreating log. An expert marksman, Coates deliberately spaced his shots in such a way that the striking force of the bullets slowly spun the log around in the water.

"Damn, these guns are fine!" he exclaimed. "We're going to give Hobst more navels than a harem full of belly dancers!"

"Yeah, well, save the showing off for the main attraction, okay?" Drago chided. He took a careful look at the latest recruits, trying to gauge their reliability. It had been a calculated risk giving them weapons in addition to Abner's money after the standoff, and so far it seemed that Drago had chosen the right course. All four of Abner's men seemed pleased with their first use of the Stealth-shooters, and none of them looked as if they harbored any bright ideas about using the guns to avenge their late boss's execution. Still, Drago didn't plan to let down his guard these last few crucial hours, even when it came to his own men. Hell, Billingsworth's defection had caught him by surprise the other night. He wasn't going to let it happen again. Especially not today.

"Okay, we've got three hours, so anybody who wants some snooze-time, now's the . . . shit!" Out on the horizon he saw a pair of growing specks headed their way. "Load up and get down!" he shouted at the others.

It didn't take long for the others to realize that a pair of helicopters were coming their way. If not part of a search crew scouring the bayous for them, Drago figured the choppers were being used to check security along the waterway in anticipation of Governor Hobst's scheduled visit to New Orleans later that day. Either way, the whirlies spelled trouble for the operation if they spent too much time taking too close a look at the land around the river bend.

The wait seemed interminable, but finally the two copters skimmed above the marshland where target practice had just been held. Drago was only a few feet away from the cabin cruiser, and if worse came to worst, he figured he'd switch to the Belgian FN long enough to bring down the choppers before making a run for it. However, the aircraft were apparently running low on fuel, or else they'd been called away on another assignment, because before they could come down to where their rotor wash might have exposed the lurking assassins, both of them banked sharply to one side and doubled back the way they'd come. In less than a minute they were back to being distant specks.

Alongside the docked cabin cruiser, Drago let out a long breath and reached for his cigarettes. He'd sure as hell be glad once this was over.

19

St. Louis Cemetery No. 1 was the oldest burial ground in Louisiana, with more than two hundred years' worth of bodies calling the grounds off Basin Street their final resting place. Some said the tombs and burial vaults were located above ground because the city sat so close to sea level that it was impossible to dig six feet down without striking water. There was some validity to the claim, but a more likely explanation had to do with customs inherited from France and Spain. In its prime, the cemetery had boasted lavish monuments to the dead, with the crypts appearing to be gigantic chess pieces on loan from Mount Olympus. Time, poor upkeep and vandals had done much to tarnish the look of the cemetery, and the grounds now held an aura of gloom and despair mirrored by the adjacent Iberville Housing Projects. Blacks predominated in the area, and by the time the funeral procession reached the so-called "city of the dead," most of the white protestors had fallen away, either of their own accord or due to the persecution of New Orleans's finest.

Cowboy Kissinger and Able Team were on hand for the final ceremony, standing alongside the slain teen's family. A burly minister offered a eulogy that dealt largely with matters of grief and personal loss. Of the four men, Carl Lyons felt the words strike home with the greatest impact. He was no stranger to funerals, and even though the customs and surroundings here were different, the sentiments were much the same. This was a time to bid farewell to someone who wouldn't be around any longer, and for the Ironman there was a long list of the dead who'd left him behind in recent years.

Lyons swallowed hard, inwardly cursing the unfairness of it all. So many good people cut loose from this world by the hand of evil. In most cases, he'd paid back the killers, life for life, but other than satisfying an urge for justice, those acts ultimately seemed inadequate. Ridding the world of anything bad never quite made up for losing a little good. The scum would always be back in some other guise that seemed somehow indistinguishable from its predecessor, but when someone good died, well, it was just different.

Fighting to keep his emotions under control, Lyons snuck a glance at his two friends and thought, fleetingly, that the day would come when one of them would be brought to a place like this inside a closed box. Or himself, for that matter. When Pol had plucked him out of the Mississippi the other night after he'd crashed the motorboat, it had been only his most recent brush with death. There had been many other times, and he knew that one day the odds were going to catch up with him, with Pol, and with Gadgets.

Yeah, and with everyone else who comes kicking and screaming from the womb, he told himself, bailing out of his reverie. Life's a bitch, and then you die. He'd said it enough times to know the score. But, fuck it, as long as that fist-sized muscle between his ribs kept pumping blood through his pain-racked body, he was going to go on living and living hard. Stay hard, as Gadgets would say.

"...and deliver us from evil," the minister intoned in his baritone voice, completing the Lord's Prayer.

"Amen," the congregation prayed in unison.

There was a moment's silence as the casket was placed into the burial vault. The dead youth's family watched on stoically. Mother, father, three surviving brothers and sisters, their taut faces strained and weary.

"G'bye, Michael," Jimmy called out as the doors to the vault were closed.

"My baby..." the boy's mother whimpered quietly, speaking as much to her slain offspring as to the youth beside her.

The band began to play "Free as a Bird," and the crowd started filing away from the burial site. Able Team stayed behind, waiting to speak with two black men in their early forties who had arrived during the middle of the funeral ceremony along with Mike Armstrong. They were standing off to one side, near a miniature stone obelisk disfigured by graffiti and pigeon droppings.

"Guys, I'd like you to meet Phil and George Hines," Armstrong said, handling the introductions. "Their brother's the one under arrest in connection with those tourist murders the other night." Mike didn't divulge the names of the Able Team members, introducing them merely as associates working for his private investigation firm.

"Luther's been framed," George insisted. "He didn't even know this boy they just buried."

"That stuff of Luther's they found by the bodies was swiped from his house," Phil Hines told them.

"You told this to the police?" Lyons asked.

George nodded. Pointing over at the grieving family, he added, "And that boy told 'em his brother said some white dude did the shooting."

"I know," Lyons said, "Are the cops buying it?"

"They say they'll look into it, but that don't mean jack shit," Phil complained. "Far as the cops are concerned, anybody named Hines in this town is a Black Panther out to play burn-baby-burn."

"Well, weren't you two with the Panthers?" Lyons asked.

"That's history, man," Phil said. "Besides, it's got nothing to do with Luther. He hung out at a few meetings with us back when he was a kid, but it wasn't for him. He's legit, and somebody's tryin' to hang a rap on him."

More pieces to the puzzle, Lyons thought to himself. Somehow this incident was linked with Drago, Crosley, the Shiites and God knows how many others. But there was an even more pressing concern that had been on his mind since the ten-year-old boy had first come to them back at the hotel.

"Mike, I need to talk to you alone for a minute," he told Armstrong.

The two men excused themselves and walked away from the others, pausing near the infamous burial vault of voodoo queen Marie Laveau, etched with crosses by those hoping a little of the dead woman's special magic might rub off favorably on them.

"Problem?" Armstrong inquired.

"Mike, you're putting people in touch with us here like we're listed in the white pages, know what I mean?"

"I know it's irregular, and I apologize," Mike told the Ironman. "But you have to realize that New Orleans is home for me, and just the past few days I've been getting bad vibes about the way things are shaping up. There's something bad brewing, Carl, and it's about to come to a head."

"I'll buy that," Lyons conceded, "but I still don't see why you have to risk our covers to—"

"Time, Carl," Armstrong interrupted. "I don't have time to take down statements, then look you up and dish it back out. As it is, right now I should be down near the Bureau office trying to keep up with their investigation, and my wife's doing overtime on the shortwave checking out the police. And none of these people are going to know anything about Stony Man or Able Team."

Carl sighed and nodded his head reluctantly. "Yeah, okay. I see your point." He glanced around, taking in the clutter of grave markers. "I guess all this dyin's just getting to me."

"I'm not surprised," Armstrong said. His belt pager started beeping again. "Well, that's Sarah. Let's hope she's come up with something we can use. I tell you, Carl, this town's turned into a powder keg, and unless we get to the fuse before it burns all the way down, there's going to be one hell of an explosion."

Armstrong went off to find a phone while Lyons rejoined Blancanales, Schwarz and the Hines brothers. The four of them were in midconversation.

"...and most of the brothers chilled out because all the heavy crap was spoilin' things," Phil was saying. "We got to figurin' that pushin' for violence was only gonna get our own asses kicked in. Luther's cool, man. No way he'd use a gun. Smooth-talkin', that's his thing."

"Well, with any luck he won't have to bother doing any of that talking in a courtroom," Blancanales said.

"You believe us, then?"

Blancanales bobbed his head. "Yeah, we believe you."

"Either of you guys ever heard of the Aryan Right Coalition?" Schwarz asked the brothers.

"Heard of 'em?" Phil Hines laughed bitterly. He pointed across the burial ground to an old, chipped vault. "We got a cousin buried over there. He woke up one night with a cross burning on his front lawn, and when he ran out to hose it down, he got a bullet through the heart. Married with four kids, and one shot takes him out. Fucking ARC called the paper the next morning lookin' to take credit for it."

"Lemme tell you something," the second brother said, anger creeping into his voice. "Mebbe I swore off takin' the violent way, but lemme get my hands on the chickenshit that pulled that trigger, he'll be dead meat...."

Mike Armstrong reappeared and took Able Team inside.

"My wife just got paid a visit by some kid she used to baby-sit for," he said.

"So...?" Blancanales responded.

"So, his name's Louis Billingsworth," Armstrong revealed. "He's the one who called the cops about the gun drop."

"He's with ARC?" Lyons asked.

"Was. Says he split before the drop went down. He wants police protection and says he'll cooperate if we give it to him."

"Does he know what Drago's up to?" Blancanales asked.

Armstrong shook his head. "Next best thing, though. Says he'll take us to their headquarters."

20

Howie Crosley slammed down the receiver in disgust. He'd tried to reach Abner Smith at three different numbers down in Mobile, but the man was nowhere to be found. His customized cabin cruiser was missing from its space at the marina as well, and the only clue to his whereabouts came from the secretary at the Mobile Shores Yacht Club, who said Smith often took his boat out for days on end and there was nothing to be concerned about.

Crosley knew better.

Smith had promised to call him once he got back from making the weapons drop in New Orleans. That had been more than forty hours ago.

It wasn't money that Crosley was worried about. Abner had paid off Cholly already with the understanding that he'd be reimbursed by ARC when the guns changed hands in New Orleans.

New Orleans.

That's what bothered Crosley. He'd read the paper and watched the news, and he knew instinctively that the tourist murders and the shitstorm on the docks were both tied to ARC and its plans for the purchased Stealth-shooters. The cops were being particularly tight-lipped about the dock incident, and Crosley's fear was that Abner had been apprehended and his boat impounded, along with the guns. If that was the case, Crosley was on thin ice. Even if Smith didn't try to save his ass by turning state's evidence, having possession of guns alone might give the law enough clues to sniff a trail back to Birmingham.

"Goddamn it all to hell!" he raged, taking out his frustration on the ceramic statue of Jefferson Davis that Senator Calhoun had given him last Christmas. One fierce swipe of his hand sent the miniature Confederate hero flying from Crosley's desk into the polished oak of the den's paneled walls. Breaking into countless shards, the statue was about as salvageable as Humpty Dumpty after he'd had his great fall.

At the wet bar across the room, Crosley tried dousing his anger with a strong shot of Wild Turkey, but the bourbon only seemed to fuel his rage. It was bad enough that he had to worry about things coming unglued for him in New Orleans. There was also Donnie's threats of blackmail here at home. The cop hadn't gotten around to asking for money yet, but Crosley was sure it would only be a matter of time.

And time, Crosley feared, was running out for him. If he was going to emerge from all this with his head above water, he was going to have to take action, and take it fast.

He went back to his desk and roamed through his Rolodex until he found Ahmed Khoury's New York number. An officious secretary tried to take a message, but Crosley insisted that it was imperative for him to speak to the attorney. After being put on hold for nearly five minutes of piped-in music, Howie heard the Muslim's accented voice on the other line.

"Yes, Mr. Grossler. What seems to be the problem?"

"The problem, Mr. Khoury, is that I'm pushing up your pickup date for the Stealthshooters." Crosley managed to sound calm, authoritative.

"Oh. To when?"

"Tomorrow afternoon."

"Impossible."

"Not if you want the guns."

"Why this change?"

"I don't ask you about your private matters, Mr. Khoury, do I?"

There was a pause. Although Khoury had apparently cupped his hand over his mouthpiece, Crosley could still hear him shouting commands in his native tongue to someone else in his room. Finally the lawyer resumed the conversation.

"Very well, Mr. Grossler. I can bend to your arrangements in this case ... provided you will agree to cut your asking price by ten percent to make up the inconvenience."

"No way, Khoury. Look, if you don't want these guns I can always sell them to Israel."

Khoury lapsed into a quick burst of choice Arabic profanity, then regained his poise and muttered, "Five percent."

"Done." Crosley proceeded to give Khoury directions to his plantation, adding, "You'll need three pickup trucks, and you can only bring in one extra man per truck."

"You are a very paranoid individual, Mr. Grossler."

"No shells on the pickups, either," Crosley went on, ignoring Khoury's comment. "Open beds on all three. I want a clear view of everyone coming onto the property."

"Why shouldn't I suspect that you are the one that is planning foul play?" Khoury inquired. "This sounds as if you want me to wander into an ambush without enough men to protect myself."

"That's a chance you'll have to take."

"I see." There was another brief pause on the line, then Khoury said, "I suppose that for my own protection I should have my men prepared to call the local authorities about your dealings with a group called the Aryan Right Coalition in New Orleans, hmm?"

It was Crosley's turn to contribute a little dead air to the conversation. Goddamn, how did Khoury know about that already? "I don't know what you're talking about," Crosley finally mumbled.

Khoury laughed in Crosley's ear. "Mr. Grossler, it was our money that ARC used to buy their guns."

"I don't believe you." Sweat broke out on Crosley's brow.

"Then perhaps you should call Mr. Drago in New Orleans and ask him about his dealings with a Mr. Peter Stevens."

Crosley had been trying to reach Drago without success since the night of the gun drop. He doubted that there was any point in trying again. It was obvious that Khoury was telling the truth, damn him.

"Okay," he told the Muslim. "I think we've established that it's in our mutual best interests to make this a clean deal."

"Good. I'll abide by your terms for the pickup. Six men, three trucks. Tomorrow afternoon."

"Three o'clock."

"Very well, Mr. Grossler. I'll see you then."

Crosley hung up the phone and swung around in his chair. Out through the window behind his desk he had a view of the plantation. Fifty sprawling, landscaped acres, filled with citrus orchards, riding stables, an Olympic-sized pool, three-hole golf course . . . all the amenities he thought should be part of the good life. It'd be a damn shame to leave it all behind. But Birmingham was becoming too hot for him. It was time to pull up stakes before the welcome mat caught fire. Once he sold the Stealthshooters to Khoury, he'd have another half million in currency to go along with the cash from Abner Smith and any other transportable valuables he could put together between now and tomorrow afternoon without drawing suspicion.

Take the money and run.

Just as Howie Crosley had become Evan Grossler, he'd leave behind this mess and set up shop somewhere else with yet another identity. To hell with Donnie, to hell with Abner and Drago.

And to hell with John Kissinger.

21

"Down there!"

Louis Billingsworth pointed out the helicopter window at a barren stretch of marshland.

"I don't see anything but a few flattened shacks," Lyons said, inspecting the terrain where the young man was pointing.

"That's the point," Billingsworth responded. "We chose each place with a lotta care to make sure it wouldn't stand out."

"Okay, then," Lyons sighed, pulling out his Colt Python and turning to George Hines, who was at the chopper's controls. "Bring 'er down."

"Will do."

The helicopter was one of three owned by George and Phil Hines as part of their air-tours business, an enterprise they'd gotten into based on the inspiration of their favorite television character, T.C., from *Magnum, P.I.* When they'd overheard Armstrong's news about a breakthrough in finding ARC, the brothers had eagerly volunteered their assistance. Given the circumstances, it had been an offer Able Team couldn't refuse. A few miles away, Phil Hines was piloting another chopper carrying Blancanales and Kissinger, using Billingsworth's markings on a topographical map of the Plaquemines Parish marshlands to aid in the search for Drago's hellsquad. A small contingent of local law-enforcement officers, including Mike Armstrong, was covering the same turf by hovercraft and on foot, but most of New Orleans's official manpower, including that of the National Guard, was relegated to keeping the peace inside the city boundaries. A number of small-scale skirmishes between races had broken out since the incident during the funeral march, and there was little indication that tensions were going to lessen in the foreseeable future.

Gadgets was the fourth passenger in George's chopper, riding in back with his M-16 clutched in his meaty palms. He turned to Billingsworth, whose ankles were cuffed to the seat in front of him. "Would they leave a man behind to stand guard if they're not here?"

"Not likely," Louis said. Despite the fact that he was under arrest and shackled, he was in a cooperative mood, eager to make up for the wrong turn his life had taken. "All their records and shit like that's back at their office in the city. Out here they always travel light and never leave much behind, so there's really not much to guard."

George Hines eased the chopper down onto a clearing thirty yards away from one of the fallen structures and left the engine running. At the risk of drawing suspicion to his claims of forsaking the violent philosophy of his black militant past, Hines had brought along his own personal weapon, an Ithaca Model 37 M&P Handgrip, the compact version of their 12-gauge shotgun. Equipped with the eight-shot twenty-inch barrel, it was a portable shitkicker of the highest order and a handy deterrent to anyone who might have ideas about robbing the brothers' tour business office, where the gun was usually kept.

Billingsworth was further bound with a second set of handcuffs and left behind as the other three men scrambled out of the chopper and promptly fanned out, with

Lyons charging up the middle, Hines on the left and Schwarz circling around to the right of the battered shell that had once been home for a family of oyster farmers.

In addition to their weapons, the three men also carried army surplus gas masks. On Lyons's signal, they slipped on the headpieces, giving them a bug-eyed, insectlike appearance. Once they had the structure surrounded, the Ironman unclipped a tear gas canister from his waist and activated the release valve before tossing it into an opening that Billingsworth had told them led to an underground room. Crouching in a two-hand firing stance, Lyons eyed the opening and waited.

Tendrils of gas floated back up from the subterranean lair, but there was no other sign of activity. Lyons couldn't hear anything going on inside the warped building, either. But that didn't cause the trio to drop their guard. With the utmost caution they moved in on their target.

Hines gestured that he wanted to go in first. Ithaca cradled in his large hands, the black gave himself a silent countdown, then suddenly charged through the cavity and down the cinder-block steps.

Nothing happened.

Lyons and Schwarz followed Hines down to the basement cubicle. Gas still lingered in an off-color fog, but the men were able to see that the area was deserted. The only sign of previous occupation was a well-worn cot folded up in one corner and an empty can of Sterno tipped on its side in the middle of the room.

"Shit," Lyons muttered through his mask as he led the others back up the steps to daylight. They returned to the helicopter, where Louis sat passively like the model prisoner he intended to be for as long as he was in custody.

"Well, that makes two strikes," Hines grumbled as he yanked off his gas mask, referring to another ARC compound they had checked out earlier.

"Sorry," Louis told the threesome.

"It's not your fault they're not here," Lyons told him as he reached for the chopper's radio controls. "After all, you wouldn't deliberately lead us out here on a wild-goose chase, would you?"

"No, of course not."

"I didn't think so." Lyons turned his attention to the radio microphone. "Red Dog Two, you out there?"

There was a crackling of static over the radio speakers, followed by the voice of Mike Armstrong. "Red Dog Two. Nothing worthwhile to report. We found some shells that'll probably match up with those stolen Belgian FNs, but that's about it. I just spoke to Sky Dog One, and they came up empty on their end, too. Over."

Lyons pounded a fist against the padding of his seat, then quickly reined his emotions in. "Okay. Just keep looking and cross your fingers. Over."

The Ironman set aside the mike and turned to Louis as George Hines brought the chopper back up into the air. "They're not at any of the places you told us about...not that it surprises me all that much. Could there be some other place you forgot?"

"I wish there was, but—" Louis cut himself short, and his face took on a pensive glow.

"But what?"

"There was one place I overheard Drago mention once, but we never went there and he never brought it up again, so I don't know if he decided to scrap it or what...."

Schwarz was intrigued. "Where?"

"Beats me," Louis told him. "Like I said, we never went there."

"But he did mention it, right?" Schwarz unfolded a topographical map and laid it out across Billingsworth's lap. "Think hard and make an educated guess."

Louis surveyed the map slowly, carefully. With his hands still bound, he wasn't able to point anymore. "Okay, if I had to guess, I'd say down there on the lower right, close by the river. I remember he said something about stalking a poacher when he found the place, right near the gator feeding grounds."

"Good job, kid." Schwarz passed the map up to Lyons and pointed out the designated area. Hines noted the locale and changed their course accordingly. Lyons picked the radio microphone back up and tuned in the appropriate frequency that put him in touch with both of the other search parties.

"All units, this is Sky Dog Two. We've got one last spot to check out. Why don't we all meet there and then figure out where to go. Stand by for coordinates."

THE OTHER CHOPPER WAS closest to the area in question, and Pol Blancanales peered through binoculars as Phil Hines slowly skimmed over an old shack built on stilts near a decrepit dock that poked out into the Mississippi.

"I see a couple of guys loading something into a hydrofoil," Pol said. "Get a little closer."

"You got it."

As the chopper banked to one side and drifted closer to the moored hydrofoil, Kissinger readied his .45 in the back seat.

"Aw, man, it's just a couple brothers," Phil said, making out the two men without need of binoculars. "Look like oyster farmers."

The men in question stopped what they were doing and warily eyed the chopper. One of them moved to the front of the hydrofoil and reached for a shotgun.

"Something tells me this guy doesn't like being a tourist attraction," Blancanales told Hines. "Let's beat it."

"Done." Phil Hines jockeyed the controls and veered his aircraft downstream from the elevated shack.

"We could have just asked if they'd seen anyone suspicious around lately," Kissinger said.

"Couldn't come any more suspicious-looking than us," Hines said. "There's no way I'm goin' back there, 'cause the only thing we'd be asking for is trouble."

Blancanales resumed his reconnaissance, then suddenly whistled low and long as he pointed through the window.

"*Madre de Dios*, I think I just lost my appetite."

Down below, on a small spit of land surrounded by several offshoots of the main river, four alligators were feasting on what had clearly once been a man.

"Looks like white meat to me," Hines said as he swung around and came in closer to the feeding ground. "This might be the place."

"I see an opening over there," Kissinger observed, pointing to a dark gash in the earth a few yards off to the right of the gators.

"We better check this out, but first let me clear the runway, okay?" Pol rummaged through a tote bag filled with a few tricks Able Team liked to carry around as a complement to their firearms. He reached past the gas masks and tear gas for a flash-bang grenade. When Hines hovered the chopper above the gators, Blancanales pulled the pin and let the device drop amid the long-bellied predators. Instead of frag and shrapnel, the grenade was packed with enough blinding flash powder and noise-maker to convince the alligators that the chopper wasn't dropping by for dessert. They abandoned what was left of Abner Smith and slithered off into the river.

The explosion, however, drew no response from the area around the opening that Kissinger had pointed out. Phil Hines set the copter down within striking distance. Blancanales and Cowboy Kissinger piled out, each man packing a .45 and a gas mask. Hines relied on his house-hold guardian, a Ruger 77/22 Rimfire rifle loaded with a ten-shot magazine of .22-caliber Long Rifle bullets. It was a weapon ill-suited for close-quarter combat, so he stayed back and covered the other two men from the rear.

Flanking either side of the opening, Kissinger and Pol donned their gas masks and followed the same siege strategy their Able Team counterparts had employed earlier. They emerged empty-handed several minutes later, by which time the other two search parties had arrived on the scene. Lyons and Schwarz were out of the first chopper, standing over Smith's grisly remains.

"Find anything besides him?" Lyons asked Blancanales.

Pol coughed a few times after taking off his gas mask. He was limping slightly, favoring his bandaged thigh. "Some litter down there, and a lot of fresh blood. Maybe had a little mutiny on the *Bounty*."

"And there was something else," Kissinger added. "A diagram on the floor of the shack. Looked like a section of the river with ambush coordinates."

"Ambush?" Lyons frowned and glanced at Mike Armstrong, who'd just walked over after getting off the police hovercraft. "You know anyone out on the river today worth being bushwhacked?"

Armstrong thought it over. His jaw suddenly clenched. He nodded grimly. "Matter of fact, there is." Unfolding the topographical map he'd been using for the past few hours, he told Pol, "Lemme borrow that mask so I can go have a look at the diagram. If I'm right, we've got a real problem on our hands."

22

The *River Queen* lived up to her regal name as she voyaged down the Mississippi, clouds of steam rising from twin smokestacks, huge stern wheel—gleaming red as the painted lips of a brothel madam—churning up the cool dark water as it urged the elegant ship onward. Meticulously restored in a successful effort to recapture the grandeur of those days when countless steamboats roamed the waters of the region, the *River Queen* was truly a symbol of the Old South. It was therefore the perfect place upon which to hold a fund-raising benefit for Louisiana Governor Hobst. Although they were only a few miles downriver from New Orleans, that city's current problems seemed far, far away, especially in the politician's address to his loyal supporters. He spoke of a beloved past, one that for the most part had been glossed over with fond memories and excised of its darker elements.

"It is time for us to turn our back on the stigma that has plagued those of us who looked upon the past with fondness," the governor told his followers, wrapping up his speech. He thumped his fist on the podium for emphasis. "There is nothing wrong with the old-fashioned values we stand for, and I daresay that if the rest of the country were to embrace those same values with the same fervor, this would be a stronger nation!"

More than three dozen contributors—industrialists, farmers, real estate barons and others who envisioned themselves part of a network of good ol' boys—had paid a thousand dollars apiece for the privilege of riding the *River Queen*, consuming lavish portions of peppersteak, jambalaya, black-eyed peas and draft beer, and hearing Hobst tell them how the South was going to rise again. They liked what they had heard so far and filled the governor's pause with enthused clapping and a few choice cries of assent.

"Hear!"

"That's tellin' 'em!"

Just a few months past his fiftieth birthday, Hobst was a man of average build with a prematurely receding hairline and pale eyes that seemed at odds with his otherwise youthful features. He dressed conservatively, and gave the overall impression of being a small-town citizen reluctantly thrust into the limelight by a sense of duty. People often remarked on his resemblance to Jimmy Stewart at a similar age. The governor's campaign staff had seized on the comparison by christening their man's White House bid "Mr. Hobst Goes to Washington," in reference to the Frank Capra film classic Stewart had starred in fifty years before. Hobst had even gone so far as to bend his Southern drawl to fit a closer approximation of Stewart's vocal phrasing, and his speeches were always given as if from the perspective of an embattled underdog taking a stand on behalf of the little man. His effectiveness was almost spooky, especially when given the fact that most of his support came from the wealthier segment of the population.

"And so, I say to you," Hobst went on after the applause had died down, "it's time that we rose to the challenge of the times and helped to lead this fine nation back onto the road of righteousness and dignity!"

"Yes!" came a cry from the back.

"Back to the wisdom of our forefathers!" Hobst exhorted.

"Right on, Governor!"

"Back to those days of glory when we as a people stood tall in the eyes of the world!" More applause erupted throughout the dining room of the *River Queen*. This time Hobst didn't wait for it to fade. He rode it like a surfer atop a long-sought wave, building his voice to a crescendo. "I beg you, citizens, as we rise to the greatness that is our destiny, let me be the one who leads you!"

Pandemonium broke out on the floor as diners rose from their seats and shouted in praise, lifted glasses for toasts in Hobst's honor and otherwise assured themselves that money spent on the governor's campaign was the best goddamned investment any of them would ever make. Hobst stepped away from the platform and began mingling with the others, shaking hands, patting shoulders and flashing his patented shy-but-charming smile.

Hakim Shrevi was among those in the banquet area. He sat calmly in his seat, sipping water from a crystal goblet as he waited for an opportune moment. From his seat he had a clear view of the Louisiana shoreline. Willows and tawny marsh grass crowded the embankments, but there was one point near a wide bend in the river where the towers of an oil refinery came into view, marking just one of countless locations along the Mississippi where energy corporations had set up shop over the years. Spotting the towers, Shrevi set down his water glass and dabbed his lips with a napkin before excusing himself from his table.

Governor Hobst had worked his way to the bar and was talking with an aide as he waited for his drink.

"Excellent speech, Governor," Shrevi told Hobst as he approached the bar, extending a hand.

"Why, thank you, Mr...."

"Stevens," Shrevi introduced himself as the two men shook hands. "Peter Stevens. I'm with the Concerned Citizens Association. I trust you received our most recent check toward your campaign."

"I'm sure we have." Hobst shot his aide a quick glance. The younger man returned a subtle nod along with a slight bit of equally discreet fingerplay that signaled to the governor that he was in the presence of a heavy contributor, one worth a little extra stroking.

"Well, then, Mr. Stevens," Hobst said as he took his ginger ale from the bartender. "What sort of suggestions would you make to help us reach our objectives?"

"As a matter of fact, I do have an idea that might interest you. It's a rather sensitive matter, however...." Shrevi let his eyes drift to take in the activity of the crowded dining facility before looking back at Hobst. "Perhaps we could discuss it somewhere less noisy. Say, out on the deck?"

"Splendid idea!" Hobst said. "I could use a breath of fresh air. Bring a drink along, why don't you?"

Shrevi asked the bartender for a soda water, then walked with Hobst toward the exit. The aide tagged along, as did a pair of Secret Service agents, part of the crew assigned to Hobst the day he had announced his candidacy. Shrevi didn't mind the others joining them, although he was somewhat wary of the government men. From the faint bulges in their suit coats he knew they were toting guns. There was a chance they could make problems for Drago.

But that was Drago's problem. All Shrevi had been asked to do was get Hobst out in the open within five minutes of passing the refinery towers, and it looked as if he was going to succeed with a couple of minutes to spare. Then all that remained would be for him to find a way to get out of the line of fire.

A LIBERAL APPLICATION of theater makeup had darkened the skin of Stan Drago and the other men crouched in the tall grass alongside the river. They were spread out on either side of the same bend where they had earlier tested their Grossler Stealthshooters on a floating log. Now they were waiting in anticipation of the arrival of the ultimate target.

Several minutes ago they had heard a blast from the *River Queen*'s shrill horn, and now, above the tops of the swaying willows, smoke from the riverboat's twin stacks could be seen rising to embrace the low clouds that had settled over the Gulf since early morning.

"Finally," Drago muttered to himself.

He'd known about Hobst's fund-raiser on the riverboat from a circular Lew Kandrell, one of ARC's nonmilitary members, had received in the mail. From there, it hadn't taken much effort to find out the ship's itinerary and set his plot in motion. He'd wanted to be able to pull the whole thing off from the inside, but when Kandrell had balked at being the bait to lure Hobst out onto the *River Queen*'s deck, Drago had found it necessary to get back in touch with Peter Stevens. He hoped to hell he wouldn't regret the move. But, as they used to say in his high school Latin class, *Alea iacta est*.

The die is cast.

Minutes from now, the steamboat would slow to round the river bend and, provided Hobst was out on deck, Drago and his men would rise from cover and cut loose with silent rounds from their Stealthshooters. Using silencers would give them a few needed seconds of confusion aboard the *River Queen*, time enough to make sure they'd nailed their man before those on the riverboat comprehended what was happening. It would also allow them to take flight before anyone could pinpoint the direction the shots had come from.

Once it was all over, the assassins would return to one of their camouflaged barracks and wait out the inevitable search parties. Then he'd slip out to make a phone call, using a ghetto accent as he claimed credit for Hobst's death on behalf of the National Committee to Combat Fascism. The odds were that somebody on the steamboat would have caught a glimpse of the dark-tinted gunmen, and his call would only verify the racial angle that the press would already be having a field day with.

As a last ploy in the frame-up, Drago dropped a few more incriminating items Coates had surreptitiously gotten his hands on when he'd burglarized Luther Hines's home—a pamphlet outlining programs of Hines's local activist group, a decorative pin with the slogan BLACK PRIDE printed over a clenched fist and a newspaper clipping from the black-run *Delta Daily* in which Governor Hobst was derided as a racist threat to all hard-fought civil rights gains made since the fifties.

When he looked back up, Drago saw the proud hull of the *River Queen* sliding into view. He quickly raised his binoculars to his eyes and adjusted the focus, then smiled slowly.

Governor Hobst was out on deck with several other men, including Peter Stevens.

"Well, Governor," Drago uttered as he lowered the binoculars and readied his Stealthshooter. "You're a sitting duck in a shooting gallery...."

"NO QUESTION ABOUT IT," Armstrong divulged once he'd returned from the ARC outpost. "That diagram jibes with the layout for Hobst's itinerary."

"Hobst?" Lyons said. "The governor?"

"Right." Armstrong turned to one of the five police-men rounding out the marshland search team. "Fill him in. I need to get to the radio, quick!"

As Armstrong rushed off in hope of spreading the alarm to the security detail aboard the *River Queen*, the officer told Able Team about Hobst's floating fund-raiser, taking place only a few miles from where they were now standing.

"Shit, it sure as hell makes sense," Lyons said, feeling the pieces fall into place. "An ambush like that using si-lencers . . . poor bastard won't stand a chance."

"Hopefully we'll get word to them in time," the offi-cer said.

"Yeah, well, I don't think we should count on that." He turned to his comrades. "Let's hit it. Any of you know how to handle a hovercraft?"

"Sí, amigo," Blancanales offered as Able Team and Kissinger rushed toward the embankment, where the versatile bayou-hopper idled in the shallow water.

"That's a police vehicle," a ranking officer reminded the foursome.

"Maybe so, but we have clearance to run this show," Lyons countered. "You guys can come in with the chop-pers."

The hovercraft was essentially a two-man vehicle, a fact Able Team quickly realized as they tried to crowd aboard. "You and me, *amigo,*" Blancanales gestured to Schwarz. "We're the lightest."

"Damn!" Lyons swore, kicking at the mud with frus-tration. "No way we'll all be able to get there in time to—"

He was interrupted by the arrival of the weathered hy-drofoil owned by the black oyster farmer. He and his partner glared at the lawmen, shotguns in hand. It didn't take more than a few seconds for them to realize that they were vastly outnumbered and outgunned.

"Who are you guys?" the farmer asked.

"Department of Transportation," Lyons cracked, beaming at the sight of the hydrofoil. "And I'm afraid we're going to have to take that little speedster of yours out for a test drive."

"OH, I'M SORRY, Governor..." Hakim Shrevi frisked himself as if trying to locate something in his coat pockets. "I must have left my notes back at the table. If you'll excuse me for just one minute..."

"Of course, Mr. Stevens," Hobst said. "I have a few things to go over with my aides, anyway."

The *River Queen* had slowed to a crawl in the muddy waters. Shrevi casually glanced at the shoreline off to the right, doing his best not to betray the jackhammer thump in his chest at the sight of a gunman rising into view amid the blond grass. He increased his gait, making a beeline for the nearest doorway. In his haste to escape the deck, he nearly collided with a suit-coated figure bolting outside.

"Outta my way!" the other man shouted as he brushed past Shrevi. The Muslim recognized the man as one of the Secret Service agents, but he'd been knocked off-balance and was unable to prevent the agent from making his way to Hobst.

"Hit the deck!" the agent warned the others as he dived headlong, tackling the governor to the floorboards a split second before the 9 mm fusillade began riddling the *River Queen* like killer termites on a feeding frenzy.

"What the devil's going on here?" Hobst demanded, bewildered at the destruction taking place around him without any semblance of gunfire.

"Just got tipped off these guys would be gunning for—" The agent who had saved Hobst paid the high price for continuing to be the governor's human shield. A ricocheting bullet drilled through his kneecap, and when he recoiled involuntarily from the pain, a second shot slammed into his midsection, destroying his bladder and kidneys.

The other agents on deck took cover and whipped out their service revolvers, looking for assailants in the brush. Downriver, they heard the growing drone of engines, and soon a hydrofoil and a pair of helicopters were rushing into view. The agents shifted their attention to the more visible targets.

"Those are ours!" the dying man next to Governor Hobst cried out. "They blew the whistle!"

"Who the fuck are they?" another of the agents wanted to know.

COWBOY KISSINGER HAD LEARNED to operate a hydrofoil ten years ago from a fellow member of his Transatlantic Solo Sailing team. His training had been on a craft with submerged foils intended for use on rugged seas, but this ship, with slanted surface-piercing foils, ran similarly enough that the weaponsmith felt in command behind the wheel by the time he and Lyons had come within view of the *River Queen*. Elevated above the waterline, reduced drag gave the hydrofoil breathtaking speed, which had allowed the men to reach the ambush scene far sooner than they could have in a more conventional motorboat.

"It's going down!" Lyons shouted over the boat's whining power plant. He grabbed his M-16 and made sure it was set on full automatic. "Slow this crate down so we can pick a few of these bastards off!"

Kissinger eased off on the throttle, at the same time banking the craft sharply to avoid colliding with the monstrous steamboat. Lyons's gaze raked the shoreline until he was able to pick out one of the gunmen, who had already drawn a bead on the hydrofoil. A noiseless round from the Stealthshooter just missed the Ironman and shattered the ship's windshield, forcing Kissinger to raise one hand from the steering wheel to shield his face from flying glass. Fortunately the V-shaped foils provided stability during turns, and the ship didn't creep out of control.

"Nice try, fucker!" Lyons roared, gunning for the sniper and wincing as the rifle bucked in his arms, prodding nerve ends throughout his bruised frame.

The gunman in the brush lost his weapon and spun slightly to one side from the impact of Lyons's return fire. He stabbed out wildly with one hand, trying to hold on to the swaying branch of a nearby willow. The limb couldn't support his weight, however, and he toppled awkwardly through the grass and down the muddy embankment before coming to rest, half in and half out of the water. The river's current gently tried to push him back ashore.

Lyons could hear Secret Service agents aboard the *River Queen* blasting away with their revolvers, and overhead the Hines brothers were steadying their choppers so that police marksmen riding with them could try to nail the enemy with their rifles.

"Take 'er around, Cowboy!" Lyons told Kissinger. "Let's try our luck on the other side!"

Kissinger nodded, speeding up momentarily to race past the frothing wake of the *River Queen*'s paddle wheel before doubling back to make a pass along the opposite shore. A spray of gunfire nicked the sides of the hydrofoil and ripped through a flotation vest dangling over the seat behind Lyons but missed the intended targets.

"Four o'clock and twenty yards in!" Kissinger yelled at Lyons, spotting one of Drago's men attempting to flee the scene. Lyons swung his rifle around and pumped the last of his magazine into the marsh grass, mowing down the would-be assassin.

"Good job, Cowboy." Lyons grinned as he reloaded. "Nice to know all that benchwork hasn't spoiled you for the field."

"Right," Kissinger said. "I still have a little brass left on my balls."

Ready for more, Lyons peered once again into the foliage. "I wonder if we got Drago yet."

THE ARC KINGPIN WAS SNAKING away from the ambush site, moving slowly and cautiously to avoid detection from the two choppers zigzagging overhead. The air was alive with gunfire, and Drago assumed that most of his men had been spotted by now and were trading shots with the law.

Damn, he thought to himself. So fucking close and then things had to fall apart. There was still a chance that Hobst had been gunned down in the first round of fire, but Drago doubted it. Even if that part of the operation had succeeded, it wasn't going to do him a hell of a lot of good if he wasn't able to get away from this damn miniarmy that had swept onto the scene like the goddamn U.S. cavalry in the last reel of a cheap horse opera.

"Wait! Don't shoot!"

Over his left shoulder, Drago traced the cry to one of Abner's men, who was standing amid a spread of marsh grass flattened by the rotor wash of an overhead chopper. The black-faced gunman had thrown down his

Stealthshooter and was holding his arms up in a gesture of surrender.

"No way you're gonna squeal on me, shitface," Drago hissed under his breath as he raised his pistol and fired four times.

The other man twitched, doing a little death dance with a look of amazement before crumbling facedown on the ground. To Drago's relief, the chopper responded by pulling up from the body and heading back toward the steamboat, leaving him with a clear run to the side channel, where the cabin cruiser was nestled and waiting in yet another willow-draped cove.

When he got to the boat, he started up the engine and quickly reloaded his gun before easing the cruiser out into open waters. He was on a passageway that ran parallel to the river but branched off into numerous offshoots a few hundred yards downstream. With both copters flying far off to his left, he felt confident that he could reach the turnoff without being seen. From there, he could gun it full throttle until he was back out in no-man's-land, where he could either weave his way to the Gulf or ditch the cruiser and make his way to a hideout on foot.

Halfway to his escape route, Drago was startled when a huge, blurring form suddenly crashed through the wall of grass on the south embankment and plopped into the water thirty yards ahead of him. It was a hovercraft, blocking his way to freedom and swinging around to face him head-on. Two men were inside the low-profile vessel, both of them armed.

"Give it up, Drago!" Schwarz called out, standing up in the hovercraft and aiming his automatic rifle at the mercenary.

"Fat chance!" Drago took aim at the hovercraft, puncturing its rubberized skirt with gunfire and forcing it lower in the water.

Deprived of its air cushion, the hovercraft lost most of its maneuverability, but Blancanales still tried to keep up with Drago, who powered his cabin cruiser close to the opposite shoreline in an effort to circle around his pursuers and win the race to the nearby channel.

"Just hold 'er steady," Schwarz told his partner as he straddled the hovercraft and propped his M-16 against his shoulder. Lining up his sights with the now-retreating cabin cruiser, Schwarz slowly guided the barrel ahead, finally pulling the trigger so that Drago would be moving into the line of fire.

Drago never made the sharp turn that would have put him through the gateway to freedom. Dead at the wheel, he lost control of the cruiser, which had only begun to slow down when it crashed into the embankment and pitched sharply onto its side. Drago was flung forward onto the ground, and the cruiser's engines sputtered to a halt as the Mississippi began pulling it down.

"Nice shot, Gadgets," Pol said.

"Yeah, how about that?" Schwarz remarked, lowering the rifle and noticing how close the hovercraft had sunk to the waterline. "Now let's get this sucker to shore before it starts playing submarine."

23

New Orleans was a media madhouse. Mike Armstrong wryly hypothesized that the city's racial tension had died down in part because would-be rioters were afraid of being caught on camera and had decided to stay home instead of roaming the streets in search of trouble.

The big story, of course, was the attempted assassination of Governor Hobst out in the marshlands of Plaquemines Parish. Hobst himself had emerged unscathed, but one Secret Service agent had died and another had been injured in the ambush, now officially attributed to the Aryan Right Coalition. Furthermore, it had been established that ARC frontman Stan Drago was responsible for the earlier tourist murders for which Luther Hines had been arrested. Police officials were speculating that ARC was attempting to link both the tourist murders and the assassination of Hobst to black extremists in an effort to increase racial tensions in a year when just such an issue was likely to play a major role in the upcoming presidential elections.

A secondary story earning considerable attention dealt with the nature of the armed group responsible for foiling the siege of the *River Queen*. Police alluded to an ad hoc strike force comprised of members from various government agencies, but word had already leaked out that Luther Hines's two older brothers, ex-black militants Phil and George Hines, had been part of an apparent civilian posse that played a vital role in tracking down the ambushers. This twist abounded in ironies that the press lapped up eagerly.

"Nice of the bros to take the heat off us," Lyons commented as he skimmed the newspaper. He, Kissinger, Schwarz and Blancanales were back aboard the same private jet that had brought them to New Orleans. The plane had just lifted off moments before, and they were now several thousand feet above the city, heading north by northeast.

"Yeah," Blancanales agreed, massaging the aches in his wounded thigh. "Of course, even if they hadn't covered for us, there's enough overactive imaginations down there to come up with other explanations for who we were. Hell, I heard one interview where some yo-yo was saying Hines had help from some Cajun voodoo man who figured out Drago was guilty by reading chicken guts and tea leaves."

"I like this one," Lyons said, reading from the paper. "'Sources close to the investigation are reportedly looking into a possible link between the older Hines brothers and a newly formed band of left-wing white marauders eager to counter the image of all survivalist-oriented organizations as offshoots of the radical right.'"

Schwarz and Blancanales roared with laughter.

"Oh, that's rich," Schwarz scoffed. "And what do they call themselves? The Bleeding Hearts?"

"No, that's what they get if they're wounded in battle," Blancanales chuckled. "Provided they bleed liberally enough, of course."

Kissinger didn't join in the merriment. He stared out the window, lost in thought. True, all things considered, they'd tied up the mess in New Orleans into a tidy knot. But for him, there were still a lot of things left to be settled.

"Hey, Cowboy, why the funk?" Schwarz asked him finally.

"Crosley's still out there somewhere," Kissinger reminded the others. "And he's still got more of my guns earmarked for the Shiites."

The weaponsmith's concern quickly subdued the cheer in the passenger cabin. As the jet cleared the cloud line and the men found themselves with a view of the setting sun, Lyons tossed aside the newspaper. "Maybe we'll have better luck back in Birmingham this time," he ventured.

"Yeah," Kissinger muttered. "Maybe so."

HOWIE CROSLEY STARED at the evening news, dumbfounded. He hadn't thought it possible, but things were going from bad to worse. The sordid details of the assassination attempt in New Orleans were taking up almost the entire newscast. Although police were trying to keep a lid on the case, the media had gotten hold of enough footage, enough witnesses and enough informed sources to give Crosley a fairly clear idea of what had happened.

Abner Smith, half eaten by alligators, had his boat commandeered by Drago and rammed into a river embankment after the ambush was thwarted. Four surviving members of the hit squad were probably putting their lawyers through overtime trying to cut deals with the district attorney. No doubt the D.A. would play one prisoner against the other until he was able to piece together enough information on ARC operations and its recently acquired weapons to spread the focus of the investigation to Mobile and Birmingham.

Crosley switched off the television but remained in his padded chair, staring numbly at the blank screen. Tomorrow afternoon seemed like an eternity away. Too much time left for too much to happen. To hell with the Shiites. He had to get out of town tonight. Yeah, that's the way it had to be. Load up as many of the Stealthshooters as he could, take what cash he had, cut his losses and run.

A phone rang on the table next to him. He stared at it, trying to will it to stop ringing. No such luck. After eight rings, he reluctantly picked up the receiver.

"Yes?"

"Well, well. I was beginning to think you were gone." It was Donnie Welch. "You wouldn't run off on me now, would you, Howie?"

"What do you want?"

"Hey, let's not be so angry. You're talking to a friend, Howie, remember?"

"What do you want?" Crosley repeated.

"My conscience has been bothering me something terrible, Howie. All day we've been getting calls and visitors. Feds, Howie. The Bureau. Alcohol, Tobacco and Firearms. Justice Department. Hell, outfits I never even heard of. All of 'em asking the same questions. Questions I got answers to, Howie. You know, I been trying to steer clear of it all, but it ain't easy. I've had to perjure myself a few times, Howie. I feel bad about it. Real bad."

"How much."

"What's that, Howie?"

"Quit calling me 'Howie,' asshole!" Crosley snapped into the receiver. He got up from his chair and carried the phone with him across the room. "How much do you want?"

"Well, you know, I talked to Grand Dragon Lucas about your generous offer on those Stealthshooters. He figures you're about halfway home as far as clearing accounts with the Klan."

"Two crates, then. That's it?"

"For the Klan, it is. Then there's me, Howie."

Crosley didn't respond. He picked the phone up and went over to the study window where he watched the moon creeping into the night sky over his plantation.

"Howie? I didn't lose you, did I?"

"I'll give you ten thousand dollars," Crosley said. "Cash. Small denominations. Unmarked."

There was a whistle on the other end of the line, then the renegade cop told Crosley, "My, my, Howie, you must be a mind reader. I was thinking right along those lines. Yeah. Cash, small denominations, unmarked bills...you're just one little decimal point off from being right on the money."

"No fucking way I'm giving you a hundred grand, Donnie," Crosley raised his voice. "Not even if I had it."

"Oh, is that so? 'Scuse me a second, Howie. I gotta talk to a friend on the other line."

Crosley was tempted to hang up, but he wanted to wrap things up with the cop, pretend to negotiate for a black-mail payment he had no intention of honoring. If he could just get the officer to agree to keep his mouth shut a few more hours, that would give him enough time to pack and skip town.

The window Crosley was standing near suddenly shattered. Howie instinctively dropped the phone and threw himself down onto the floor. A few more pieces of glass tinkled to the floor, then there was silence. The man shifted slightly, remaining prone on the floor as he glanced over his shoulder and saw a bullet hole in the wall across from him.

"A hundred grand, Howie," Welch advised Crosley over the fallen receiver lying on the floor. The lazy mirth was gone from the cop's voice. "And don't get any ideas about leaving town without paying off. We're watching you.''

Crosley was shaking. He slowly picked up the receiver, trying to think fast. "Okay," he told Donnie. "Okay. I can have the money for you by tomorrow afternoon. Come by the plantation around three. You can get the guns for the Klan then, too."

"That's a boy, Howie. We'll see you then." Welch hung up, and Crosley heard a dial tone taunting him.

"Fuck." He set the receiver aside and turned off all the lights in the study before inching his way back to the window. Staring out, he looked over the grounds, wondering where the shot had come from. There were dozens of tall Southern pines adjacent to his property. Any one of them could have served as a sniper's nest. Donnie probably had a few Klansmen posted around the plantation now, Crosley figured. He was basically a prisoner on his own estate.

And tomorrow was visiting day. He'd deliberately scheduled things so that the Shiites and the Klan would be showing up at the same time. He wasn't sure what would happen then, but it was his hope that enough hell would erupt to give him a chance to escape.

24

"Maybe now that we've posted a reward some tongues will loosen up and we can finally make some headway."

This was the only promising news FBI Agent Ross Coe had to offer Able Team when they dropped in at the Bureau's Birmingham offices the following morning. He wasn't any more thrilled about dishing it out than the four men from Stony Man were about receiving it.

"That's it?" Schwarz exclaimed.

"Afraid so," Coe conceded. "Hell, with so goddamn many lawmen tripping over each other's toes out here trying to be the first ones to break the case, it's no wonder we can't get any cooperation. I know I'd be scared off by the thought of being run through the damn gauntlet if I came forward."

"This sucks," Blancanales said.

"My sentiments exactly," Coe said. "But that's the way it is. I gotta get back. If there's a breakthrough, I'll get to you pronto."

"We won't hold our breath," Schwarz promised.

Kissinger was on the phone, and after Coe left the room, he hung up and joined the others. "Kurtzman's been on the computers nonstop, and he hasn't had any luck, either. But Bolan called in from New York and said Ahmed Khoury's split town."

"He's on his way here, no doubt," Schwarz said, anger rising in his voice.

"Anything from Manning?" Blancanales asked.

"He says it doesn't look like any of the guns have made it out to the Middle East yet," Kissinger reported. "So there's a chance we still have time to nix the deal."

"Right, and there's a chance the Vatican might elect a pope who's not Catholic," Schwarz groused. "Fuck it, I'm going out. Maybe if I hit enough bars I'll overhear something from somebody who's had one too many."

"Just make sure it isn't you," Blancanales advised.

"Why don't you tag along and keep an eye on me, then?"

"Good idea, homes."

Schwarz and Blancanales grabbed their coats and headed out the door. Kissinger wandered over to his workbench and looked over the disassembled QA-18. "Stealthshooter," he whispered under his breath.

"What's that?" Lyons said.

"Billingsworth said Drago kept calling these guns Stealthshooters instead of QA-18s. Not a bad name, actually."

Lyons came over to the bench and looked over Kissinger's shoulder at the pistol. "My money says you've already figured out half a dozen ways to fine-tune the bastard."

Kissinger smiled. "Four ways, actually." He went on to demonstrate how he'd change the weapon. Less bulk in the handle, a slightly longer barrel, a more responsive spring mechanism in the mode switch, a whole different type of flash suppressor. "And, of course, I'd see to it that they were put together with a little more care."

"That goes without saying, doesn't it?" Lyons gave Kissinger a friendly jab in the ribs, then stepped over and picked up the spec sheets for the FOG-M missile system. "Go ahead and do your thing, Cowboy. I think I'll just look this over awhile. Never know when I might have to be the one using the sucker, right?''

Kissinger nodded absently, already absorbed in his work. He'd managed to get a look at virtually every one of the Stealthshooters that had so far been confiscated by the law, and despite his disgust at the use they'd been put to, from a purely gunsmithing perspective he was encouraged by their performance. None of the pistols had misfired, poorly constructed as they were. And with the modifications he had in mind, he was sure that ballistically the QA-18 could be made into a weapon with greater punch and accuracy than the version his former partner had put out.

''Damn, that's got to be it!'' Lyons cried out.

Kissinger glanced over at the Ironman, who was seated a few yards from the bench. The plans for the FOG-M were on his lap, and it didn't appear as if he'd so much as looked at them yet. He seemed to be responding to an inner flash of inspiration.

''Come again?''

Lyons rose from his seat and eyed Kissinger excitedly. ''That first day we were here and I was riding out to the zoo,'' he recalled, ''I remember that Welch asshole making some smartass remark about not wanting to catch the serial killer because he was doing such a good job killing blacks.''

''Yeah, you mentioned that before.''

''And yet, once we were at the zoo and we had the guy caught and spilling the beans, this same Welch guns him down.''

''He said he thought the guy was making a break for it.''

''Hah!'' Lyons scoffed. ''We both know that was a crock.''

Kissinger took a step away from the workbench. "Just what are you getting at?"

Lyons started pacing the room. "Suppose Welch shot the killer to keep him from talking?"

"You think they knew each other?"

"Okay, maybe it's a long shot, but it makes sense. Look, the guy was telling us how he surprised three guys in a back alley near a bar the night he got the guns. One of the guys was Crosley. We never got to hear a description of the others. Why?"

"Because Welch shot him," Kissinger admitted. "But, come on, Ironman, he was too far away to know what the guy was talking about."

"If he was one of the guys in the alley that night, he wouldn't want the killer talking to anyone, period," Lyons deduced. "And remember how the killer said all he could remember about that bar he was drinking in was that its name had something to do with cows? Like the Bull Bar?"

"Yeah, but…" It was Kissinger's turn to see the light. "The Oxbow!"

"Give that man a Kewpie doll!"

Kissinger snapped off the light over his workbench. "Screw the Kewpie doll," he said, "I want to get my hands on that low-life cop and shake him till the truth comes out."

IT WAS DONNIE WELCH'S DAY OFF from work, and just as well. He'd tied on a good one the previous night, painting the town red with Grand Dragon Lucas himself and a few other ranking Klansmen. Things were looking up for him in the organization, better, in fact, than they were on the force. With the Klan you didn't have to take the fucking exams and orals if you wanted a promotion.

You just took a little initiative and showed the big boys that you could play in their league.

Despite all the fuckups that had tarnished this whole business with the Stealthshooters, Welch was confident that he could emerge from it all, not only smelling like a rose, but also scoring enough points with Lucas to earn his way into the coveted inner circle. And, man, once he was there he'd be a real player. A mover and shaker. No need to put in time for the boys in blue, getting his ass blasted by street punks and having to kowtow to the fucking niggers because Durango was so goddamn worried about alienating possible voters if he ever got around to running for mayor. No, sir. Get the damn Klan behind you and you could call a spade a fucking spade.

Plodding from his bedroom, the lean man readied a pot of coffee and started it perking before retreating to the bathroom for a shave and shower. He had to go easy with the razor, since his face was still tender as hell from the drubbing that yahoo G-man had given him in the alley behind the Oxbow the other night. Just thinking about that encounter made Welch's blood boil. What he wouldn't give for a chance to get back at those uppity bastards, show 'em a few tricks the Klan had up its sleeve when it came to teaching folks their proper place. Give blondie a cattle-prod enema and see how tough he'd talk.

Done shaving, Donnie adjusted the pulse control of the shower head until the water came out in concentrated blasts. He dropped his towel and stepped under the cascade that quickly felt like hot liquid hands massaging the tight muscles in his back. He relaxed slightly and started humming to himself, impressed with the resonance his voice had when echoing off the walls of the shower stall.

Welch was about to launch into another verse of his favorite Dixie song when he suddenly became aware of another presence in the bathroom. Over the splashing of the shower, he could hear a faint, rhythmic sound. Clapping. Then a voice, somehow familiar.

"Very good, Donnie. You're no Charlie Daniels, but there's definite promise there."

Through the grimy plastic of the shower curtain, Welch saw the outline of three men. Naked and defenseless, the cop instinctively put one hand over his privates and used the other to grab the faucet.

"Let me do that for you, friend," Lyons said as he parted the shower curtain and reached for the faucet. He didn't turn it, but rather closed off the valve directing water up to the shower. Now the water poured out through a lower spigot and began filling the tub once Lyons plugged the drain.

Donnie didn't do anything to stop Lyons because Pol Blancanales had a .45 pointing in his face. In the background, Gadgets picked up a small radio from the bathroom counter. He turned it on, carrying it over to the tub until the electrical cord was stretched to its limit.

"What are you doing here?" the cop demanded. "How did you find me?"

"Tell you what, Donnie, why don't you let us ask the questions," Lyons said calmly as he stood up.

"Go to hell!"

"Yeah, we probably will," Lyons confessed. "But if you don't play along, you'll be going there first."

The water was creeping up past Donnie's ankles. Schwarz held the small radio out over the tub. It was playing an upbeat country song, something about how this guy's gal was sweet as saccharine and just as artificial.

"Careful, there," Blancanales warned Gadgets nonchalantly. "You wouldn't want to drop that in the tub and turn our friend here into a French fry, would you?"

"Gee, gosh, no," Schwarz said, pretending to lose his grip so that the radio fell from his hands. He caught the cord, however, and the appliance jerked to a stop several inches above the waterline. "Oops."

Donnie almost fell down trying to squirm clear of the radio. Fear and embarrassment had turned his flesh an interesting shade of pink.

"Stay put, *amigo*," Blancanales advised the cop, pulling back the hammer on his .45.

"This is illegal," Welch whined, starting to shiver as the cool room temperature worked over his wet skin, raising goose bumps.

"Naw," Lyons countered. "This is just a new form of therapy. It's all the rage in California now. Sort of a modified sense-deprivation tank."

"Right," Blancanales chimed in. "Get a few choice volts running through you and you'll be deprived of all your senses. So peaceful..."

"Cut it out," Donnie said. "What do you want to know?"

Lyons reached for his shoulder holster and pulled out one of the Grossler Stealthshooters for Welch to see. "You were meeting with Howie Crosley to make a deal for these when the preacher dropped in and spoiled the party. Right?"

"I don't know what you're talking about."

Lyons leaned over long enough to switch off the cold faucet. Steam rose from the spigot as unadulterated hot water poured into the tub. Lyons pulled the plug to drain off some of the lukewarm water. Donnie could quickly feel the rise in temperature around his feet.

"Soup's on," Lyons said.

It didn't take long before Donnie was finding it difficult to stand in the scalding water. He looked down at the

steaming water, then at the radio Gadgets was still holding over the tub by its cord, and lastly at the guns Lyons
and Blancanales had trained on him. "All right, all
right!" he told Able Team. "I'll talk."

25

Donnie's second vehicle, a mud-splattered Ford pickup, rolled down the paved road leading to Heavenly Acres, the plantation owned by the man Birmingham knew as Evan Grossler. The man behind the wheel drove slowly, peering out at the surrounding dogwoods, trying to pick out the Klan gunmen that were supposed to be posted in the taller trees, armed with Beeman/Krico 650 Super Sniper rifles. The man was able to spot two of the marksmen and, if his information was correct, there were four others out there somewhere.

The driver was John Kissinger, wearing Welch's clothes, down to the cop's favorite Crimson Tide ball cap and mirrored surface sunglasses. There was a vague facial resemblance between the two men, and sitting behind a dirty windshield helped his disguise.

The real Donnie Welch was going to see life from the other side of the bars.

Kissinger was wired for sound, as was the pickup itself. He was glad, because when he honked the horn at the entrance to the plantation and the wrought-iron gates slowly opened as if of their own volition, he felt as if he were driving through a set of opened jaws into the maw of death.

But at least he wasn't going in alone.

NEXT TO HEAVENLY ACRES was a wide, barren field that once a week was transformed into the site of Trade Day, Alabama's version of the swap meet. The locals would show up with a diverse and often odd assortment of items that they hoped to barter with their neighbors and entre-preneurial out-of-towners. Now that it was late in the afternoon, the shrewder bargain hunters were descending upon the field, figuring to strike choice deals with traders who'd been unable to peddle their goods for a favorable price earlier.

The field was choked with large vehicles, ranging from old buses and camper vans to five-ton trucks and a couple of semis. Some of the rigs had come from as far away as Bessemer and Talladegna, so there were plenty of strangers in addition to local folk. As such, little attention was paid to a pair of unmarked vending trucks that looked as if they had been used for dairy deliveries in a previous life. Approaching from different directions, the two trucks slowly rolled over the numerous ruts in the field before backing in to a stop near an overgrowth of wild raspberry set off behind the other vehicles.

Two dressed-down undercover police officers emerged from each truck, drawing a few brief stares from those gathered around the other vehicles. Once the men fell in with the crowd and went through the motions of barter-ing for farming implements and some peculiar-looking knickknacks made out of shellacked corncobs, they were accepted without suspicion and no one bothered to keep an eye on the trucks they'd left parked near the brush.

The rear doors of the larger truck slowly opened, and with quiet precision a dozen of the same men who had taken part in the siege at the zoo days before crept off into the brush, wearing bulletproof vests under their SWAT outfits and carrying police-issue shotguns and

service revolvers. They were bound for the Southern
pines that surrounded Heavenly Acres.

Captain Durango was among the men, determined to
show the Feds that he and his force were capable of
cleaning up their own backyards. Nonetheless, he was
secretly grateful that FBI Agent Coe and his four sidekicks had stopped by the station to tip him off about
what was going down here today.

Gadgets Schwarz and Pol Blancanales were inside the
smaller truck, which was normally used for moving and
heavy-duty maintenance chores and was accordingly
equipped with certain modifications that suited Able
Team's specific needs. Schwarz was double-checking the
FOG-M missile system to make sure it was operable. The
missile itself was rigged onto a portable launchpad in the
back of the truck. The pad, in turn, rested on a hy-
draulic lift capable of extending upward as far as two feet
beyond the retractable roof.

After he slid the roof panel aside, Schwarz took up
position before the missile's control station. He turned on
the video monitor and focused in on the missile's view of
the Birmingham sky visible through the gap in the roof.
Above the monitor, Schwarz had propped an aerial photo
of Heavenly Acres, which gave him a clear idea of the
layout of the plantation. One of the benefits of the FOG-
M was that its course could be altered appreciably while
in midflight, but when all hell was breaking loose,
Schwarz didn't want to lose any time having the missile
sniff around for its target like a bloodhound in a strange
field. Placing his right hand on the control's joystick,
Schwarz took a deep breath and let it out slowly. He
hoped Kissinger had gone over this contraption thor-
oughly enough. The idea of having the missile misfire and
blow up inside the truck somehow didn't appeal to him.

"Well, Pol, ready when you are."

Blancanales was eavesdropping on Kissinger through a pair of headphones. On Schwarz's signal, he reached over and flicked on a speaker switch so Gadgets could listen in as well.

"Coast seems clear so far," Kissinger said as he headed down the long driveway and admired the landscaped grounds. If this spread truly belonged to Crosley, he'd sure taken a step up in the world from his former digs back in Wisconsin.

"Wait, I see somebody up on my right." Kissinger quickly tried to gauge distances, knowing that Schwarz was attempting to follow his progress on the aerial photograph. "He's almost at the end of the driveway, between the mansion and the stables."

The gunsmith turned up the collar on his coat as he drew nearer to the man standing near the driveway. It definitely wasn't Crosley.

"Looks like the butler," he reported, eyeing the man's outfit. Kissinger slowed down and opened his windshield a crack. He waited for the other man to speak, watching him carefully through the mirrored lenses for signs of suspicion.

"Good afternoon, Mr. Welch," the butler told Kissinger, falling for the masquerade. "Mr. Grossler is on the phone at the moment. He said to go ahead to the workshed and he'd meet you there."

Kissinger nodded and drove on, wondering where the hell the goddamn workshed was supposed to be. He waited until he was out of the butler's line of vision then quickly glanced down at his copy of the aerial photo.

It's probably that small building in the upper right, he thought aloud as he followed a bend in the driveway toward a deserted corner of the plantation. He breathed a little easier when he saw a riding lawnmower outside the small wooden structure and an elongated pruner's pole propped up against the wall. Once he was within two dozen yards of the building, he brought the pickup to a stop but left the engine running. He remained inside the truck and quickly reported his position to Schwarz. Out past the shed, he could see a row of pines marking the property line. Up in the higher branches was another Klan sniper. Donnie had said their orders were to stay put until the deal had gone down and he'd given them a signal to give up their vigil over the plantation. On the other hand, if it looked as if Crosley was trying to pull something, they were to start firing to cover Welch's ass. Kissinger hoped the Klansmen knew how to follow orders.

AHMED KHOURY RODE at the head of his three-vehicle procession. As they approached the entrance to the plantation, he glanced out at the townsfolk gathered in the adjacent field for Trade Day. His initial suspicion that they were a front for some sort of double cross was quickly dismissed once he took a good look at the people and their collection of wares. Peasants, he thought. Fools with simple pleasures. He'd heard and read about them often from his lavish suite in New York. The common people who live off the fat of the land, rutting through one another's trash in the shadows of a decadent landowner's plantation. That's America, he thought cynically.

The gates to Heavenly Acres parted to admit Khoury and his entourage. The three pickups went through the same ritual as Kissinger, heading up the driveway and then being diverted by the butler to the workshed. Like Kissinger, the three drivers followed directions without incident. They outwardly gave every indication that they

intended to carry out the transaction for the Stealthshooters according to Crosley's guidelines. But, inside the
vehicles, each of the six men in the convoy had an Uzi
submachine gun within easy reach, not as a standard
precaution, but because they planned to use them. Once
Crosley had turned over the guns he would have out-
lived his usefulness to the Hizbullah, and as such he
would have to be eliminated so that he wouldn't get any
ideas about going to the authorities with what little he
knew about Ahmed Khoury. Furthermore, in Khoury's
opinion, anyone who so much as hinted at doing business with the jackals of Israel deserved to die, and for
that reason alone he hoped to be the first one to pump
Crosley with lead from a weapon ironically made by
those same jackals.

"LOOKS LIKE COMPANY," Kissinger said when he spotted the three pickups coming to join him near the
workshed. "I can't get a real clear view of them, but my
money says its Shiites. Gadgets, I hope you have begin-
ner's luck with that missile."

The other vehicles circled around the truck Kissinger
was in and came to a stop in a close formation, ready to
head back the way they'd come without having to bother
shifting into reverse.

"They're lining up for a quick getaway," Kissinger reported. "Make it thirty yards southeast of the shed."

No one got out of the three pickup trucks until a lone
figure strode into view from a path that wound through
the orchard between the mansion and the shed. Howie
Crosley had a key in his hand, and as he strode past the
parked vehicles, he gestured that he was going to open the
door to the shed.

"I'll be damned," Kissinger whispered. "It *is* him."

Crosley unlocked the shed door and slowly pulled it open, revealing a chest-high stack of neatly piled wooden crates. Despite his slight tan he looked pale with fear and fatigue, not unlike the way Harlan Carruthers had looked several days before when his deluded dreams had come crashing down around him. He stood to one side of the doorway and waved for the men in the pickups to come and help themselves.

Khoury's men got out first and headed for the shed, making no effort to conceal their weapons. Crosley gave no sign of being upset or even surprised at their being armed. Khoury remained near his truck, content to supervise the transfer of Stealthshooters without working up a sweat. Kissinger stayed behind the wheel of his Ford, unsure of his next move. He whispered a quick report to Schwarz that the Muslims were packing Uzis.

"Who is your friend?" Khoury asked Crosley, nodding his head in the direction of Donnie's pickup.

"Oh, him?" Crosley said, grinning sickly. "That's David Rosen. He's here to buy a few things once you're finished."

"A Jew?" Khoury exclaimed, glaring dumbfounded in Kissinger's direction. "You said you would make no deals with the Israelis!"

"What can I say, Ahmed?" Crosley shrugged his shoulders and smirked. "He twisted my arm."

Khoury shouted in Arabic to his men, who promptly set down the crates they had been preparing to move. They came up with their Uzis and started for Kissinger's truck.

"It's showtime!" Kissinger cried out, elbowing the small window behind him before diving across the seat to avoid the hail of gunfire that soon came thundering through the front windshield.

In the rear bed of Donnie's Ford, a supposedly inert blob of poorly folded tarpaulin came to life. Carl Lyons emerged from underneath the covering with Kissinger's fine-tuned Barrett M-82 in his hands. Even before he had the huge rifle's stabilizing bipod positioned on the roof of the Ford, he was already firing .50-caliber rounds at the Shiites.

"Have some lead for lunch, fellas!" Lyons howled.

Propelled with the muzzle velocity of more than twenty-eight hundred feet per second and pounding home with a wallop that measured roughly twelve thousand foot/pounds, the bullets tore into the Muslim pack like bowling balls set loose on tenpins. Lyons scored a split, gunning down the two middle gunmen. The survivors scrambled for cover inside the workshed, chased by slugs from the .45 Kissinger came up firing.

OUT ON THE PERIMETER of the plantation, Frank Chushster watched the unfolding melee through his rifle's sniperscope.

"What the hell?" he muttered incredulously. He didn't know what the goddamned Ay-rabs were doing down there, and he didn't know who the hell that was taking potshots from the back of Donnie's pickup. All he knew for sure was that he was supposed to be keeping Donnie from getting his ass blown to bits, and toward that end he trained his sights on one of the Muslim gunmen visible inside the workshed.

"Freeze!"

The command came from down below. Frank eased his finger off the trigger and looked down at the base of the oak tree. Two men had guns pointed at him. One of them was flashing a badge.

"You're under arrest!"

Frank briefly reflected on his options. He might be able to nail one of the cops, but the other would be able to pick him off with no problem, since he was, in every sense of the word, up a tree.

"Shit," he grumbled.

"Drop the rifle!"

"Oh, come on, man!" Frank whined. "Can't you appreciate a good gun when you see it? I drop this baby, it'll be ruined."

"Drop the gun and get your ass down here before I shoot it off!"

Frank sighed. As he prepared to give himself up, he saw another one of his fellow Klansmen already being led away in handcuffs. So much for their sniper's holiday.

THE FOG-M'S LAUNCHING PAD had been elevated through the truck's roof. Schwarz mouthed a silent countdown and fired the missile. The truck shook, and Gadgets stared with amazement as he followed its two-hundred-mile-per-hour course on the monitor and used the joystick to control which direction it flew on its fiber-optic tether.

"This is fucking unreal, homes," Blancanales said as he stared over Schwarz's shoulder.

"The future, my friend."

They saw the plantation on the screen, and Schwarz fiddled with the joystick, veering the missile closer to the corner of the estate where the fighting still raged. Both men could hear gunfire over the speakers broadcasting transmissions from Welch's pickup.

"If you're out there, Gadgets," Kissinger's voice crackled over the sound of gunfire, "take out the whole damn workshed!"

"Your wish is my command," Schwarz said with a grin as he homed the missile in on the target.

Kissinger and Lyons stayed near the Ford as they continued to trade shots with the enemy. They were having problems holding the men in the shed at bay, and with their attention divided, they lost track of both Khoury and Crosley. The lawyer managed to scramble into his pickup and drive off, while Crosley broke into a mad run for the orchard.

Lyons was reloading the M-82 when he spied the red blur of the FOG-M heading for the shed.

"Down, Cowboy!" he shouted as he flattened himself against the bed of the pickup.

Kissinger had crawled out of the Ford and was firing from behind the right front fender. He dove to the dirt on Lyons's command and felt the earth shake beneath him as the FOG-M lived up to its claim of stunning accuracy. Striking the workshed by way of the opening, the missile exploded on impact with the crates of Stealthshooters, creating an earsplitting blast that obliterated the shed and everything within a ten-foot radius around it. Shrapnel, some of it Muslim flesh, flew out in all directions, denting the sides of the Ford and rattling the pickup as if it were made of balsa.

"You all right, Cowboy?" Lyons asked as he jumped down from the back of truck, his ears still ringing from the explosion.

"Yeah, fine."

"One of them got away," Lyons said, jumping into the driver's seat of the Ford. The Uzis had ventilated the pickup considerably, but it still ran.

"Help yourself," Kissinger said, starting off on foot. "I'm going to get Crosley."

AHMED KHOURY DROVE wildly from the war zone. In his haste, he overshot a turn and left the driveway, plowing through a bed of camellias. By the time he spun his way out of the soft soil and back onto the roadway, Lyons was already coming up behind him.

Urging himself on with a stream of epithets, Khoury floored the accelerator, putting more distance between his pickup and the Ford. As he turned onto the last stretch leading to the main road, he suddenly braked, seeing a police car coming onto the property, beacon lights flashing on its roof. His pickup skidded sideways, crashing through a hedge and continuing to spin out of control until it skidded across a patch of concrete and toppled into the deep end of the plantation's massive pool, which had been drained for the winter and provided little cushion to break the vehicle's fall.

Lyons was the first on the scene, ready with his Colt Python to finish off Khoury. It wouldn't be necessary. The attorney was pinned underneath the vehicle, his body twisted in a way that no spine could withstand without snapping like a candy cane.

"Nice dive, ace," Lyons told the dead man. "I'd give it a nine-four."

A CHANCE!

There's still a chance!

Crosley ran with the delirious abandon of a madman, whisking through the orchard toward the back edge of the property. If he could make it that far, he could slip through the hedges and . . .

A gunshot sounded behind him at virtually the same moment he felt something slam into his hip with so much force that he lost his balance and sprawled headlong onto the ground, landing near the base of an orange tree.

There was fallen fruit all around him. He reached for his hip, only now beginning to feel an inkling of pain. When he pulled his hand away, there was blood on his fingers. He started to laugh.

Kissinger walked up to Crosley and stared down at the wounded man.

"Hey, John," Crosley cried out gaily. "Long time, no see, buddy."

"Get up!"

Crosley continued to laugh. He picked up one of the oranges and stared at it like Hamlet ogling Yorick's skull. "Say, did you ever hear the story of how blood oranges got their name?" he asked Kissinger. "There was this general at a fort near here who had ordered his men to stay in their barracks while he was in town to visit the President. When the general got back and found out that one of the men had snuck off to visit a local whore-house, he ordered the man court-martialed. They stood him up in front of an orange tree and shot him. The next year the oranges had red streaks in them."

"Get up, Crosley!" Kissinger demanded again.

Crosley shook his head and laughed some more, then suddenly lunged forward and started to heave the orange at Kissinger as he pulled a gun from its holster in the small of his back. Cowboy pulled the trigger first.

Crosley fell dead at his one-time partner's feet. He dropped the gun, but the orange was still in his hand. Kissinger knelt over the man and took the orange from his fingers. He peeled it.

No red streaks.

EPILOGUE

"I understand congratulations are in order."

John Kissinger looked up and saw Hal Brognola in the doorway, watching him as he toyed with one of his ever-present cigars. The weaponsmith was in the den at Stony Man headquarters, enjoying a mug of coffee before a blazing hearth. Outside, snow fell over the Virginia compound. It had been two weeks since the debacle at Heavenly Acres.

"How's that?" Kissinger asked the chief.

"Kurtzman tells me you just sold the patent for your Stealthshooter."

"Oh, that."

"Yeah, that."

Kissinger finished his drink and set his mug on a table between the two men. He watched Brognola gaze into the fire and chew contemplatively on his cigar. "Something on your mind, chief?"

Brognola shrugged. "Must have made a pretty penny on that deal, eh?"

"What, for the patent?"

"Yeah, the patent."

"I came out okay."

Brognola placed the cigar on a small ceramic tray on the table. He wondered aloud, "I suppose that you re-tained some kind of control over the gun, hmm? Some kind of consultant position, maybe even a spot on the board of executives..."

Kissinger chuckled and shook his head. "Look, chief. All the money's going into a trust fund. I get a little spare change every month and my mother gets her house payments taken care of. The rest is just going to sit around and draw interest for the time being."

"Oh, I see." Brognola raised an eyebrow. "And what about this firm that bought the patent for your gun?"

"They own it, lock, stock and barrel. The only input I have is if they want to make any changes in the basic design."

"You weren't offered a position?"

"Well, I was, actually." Kissinger grinned with amusement at Brognola's discomfort, letting the older man squirm a few beats longer before adding, "Of course, I turned them down."

"Ah, turned 'em down, did you?"

"Yeah, chief. You see, I already have a good job."

Brognola sighed. "I, ah, guess that means you're sticking around at Stony Man a while longer."

"Yep," Kissinger said. He got up from his chair and grabbed the notepad he'd been scribbling on before Brognola's arrival. "As a matter of fact, chief, I've figured out a couple more things I want to try out with the Barrett. If you'll excuse me, I think I'll be heading back to my shop to see if they'll work."

"Well, I surely won't stop you," Brognola replied, easing back in his chair and propping his feet on the table. He looked as if a great burden had been lifted off his shoulders. "Maybe you'd be a good chap and toss another log on the fire for me, eh, Cowboy?"

"Sure thing, chief."

Kissinger added a nice chunk of pine to the blaze, then nodded a farewell to Brognola on his way out of the room. Before leaving the farmhouse, he stopped off in the kitchen, where the three members of Able Team were seated around a table, drinking beer over bowls of hot, steaming chili.

"Okay, I admit it," Lyons was telling Blancanales, "this batch rates right up there with the stuff my Uncle Floyd used to make."

"I'll take that as a compliment," Pol said. He noticed that Gadgets had broken out into a fit of laughter. "What's so funny, *amigo*?"

It took a few seconds for Gadgets to bring his laughter under control. Then he told Blancanales, "The Ironman's Uncle Floyd got sent upriver for trying to kill his wife by putting rat poison in her chili."

"What?" Blancanales turned to Lyons. "Is that true?"

"Of course not," Lyons insisted, although when he turned to acknowledge Kissinger, he winked conspiratorially. "Hey, Cowboy, how's about joining us?"

"Thanks, but I'm gonna stay out of this," Kissinger told the trio.

"Oh, come on, pull up a chair and grab a brew," Schwarz said. "We're just kidding Pol. This stuff ain't half bad, really."

"Critics!" Pol sneered. He eyed Kissinger like an overzealous mother and pointed to the serving bowl of chili in the center of the table. "Try it, you'll like it."

"Okay, okay." Kissinger took a beer from the refrigerator and sat down with the other three men, who had fallen back into their petty bickering. Cowboy smiled. It was like being at the family table.

JAMES AXLER

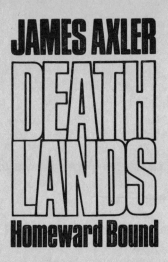

DEATH LANDS

Homeward Bound

**In the Deathlands,
honor and fair play are words of the past.
Vengeance is a word to live by . . .**

Throughout his travels he encountered mankind at its worst.
But nothing could be more vile than the remnants of Ryan's
own family—brutal murderers who indulge their every whim.

Now his journey has come full circle. Ryan Cawdor is about
to go home.

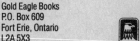

TAKE 'EM NOW

FOLDING SUNGLASSES FROM GOLD EAGLE

Mean up your act with these tough, street-smart shades. Practical, too, because they fold 3 times into a handy, zip-up polyurethane pouch that fits neatly into your pocket. Rugged metal frame. Scratch-resistant acrylic lenses. Best of all, they can be yours for only $6.99.

MAIL YOUR ORDER TODAY.

Send your name, address, and zip code, along with a check or money order for just $6.99 + .75¢ for postage and handling (for a total of $7.74) payable to Gold Eagle Reader Service. (New York and Iowa residents please add applicable sales tax.)

Remove from pouch...

unfold once...

GOLD EAGLE Gold Eagle Reader Service
901 Fuhrmann Blvd.
P.O. Box 1396
Buffalo, N.Y. 14240-1396

unfold twice...

and they're ready to wear.

GES-1A

Offer not available in Canada.